Copyright © 2021 by Michael James

All rights reserved.

No part of this book may be reproduced in any form or by any electronic or mechanical means, including information storage and retrieval systems, without written permission from the author, except for the use of brief quotations in a book review.

Grandma's Silent Auction
December
BY: Michael James

CHAPTER ONE
CIARA

I spent the last four days with my newfound family. I tried my damndest to be in the moment with them. I took my father, Molena, Celine, and Brock to my store before we hit the rest of the city for Christmas shopping the day after Thanksgiving. We went to the movies the next day, then Grams and I introduced them to Red Fox where we had a lot of wine afterward. We basically chilled at Grams' enjoying each other's company the rest of the time. I got to know them all better. It's still hard to believe I know who my father is, let alone knowing I have a half-sister. I enjoyed every minute I had with them all. As I said, I did my damndest to be in the moment, it was always on my mind that I have no idea what happened with Kaiden. I tried to call him quite a few more times. It's upsetting to say the very least that I haven't been able to reach him. I don't understand why he wouldn't even return my calls. I don't know if I should be worried about him or if I should take the hint that he wants nothing to do with me. My heart isn't ready to give up; I know I cannot move on without knowing which one it is. I am going to find him if it's the last thing I do, that is why I booked a flight to Vegas for later today. I packed a bag right after my family left this morning. I am unsure how many days I'll be gone, so I stuffed as many clothes in my suitcase that I could fit into it. I do know I can't move forward with not knowing if he ever really loved me or not.

I glance at my phone when it rings and Malcolm's name appears. I have been avoiding his calls ever since I talked to him two days before Thanksgiving. He called me that day to let me know his trip was delayed a day. Therefore, he wasn't getting home until that Wednesday night. Malcolm had invited me to come spend the holiday with his family, but I told him I couldn't. He understood since it was short notice. I've been avoiding him because I've been busy with my family. Plus, I don't know what to say to him. When all my focus isn't on Kaiden, I do plan to see him. Malcolm has shown me a ton of respect and I plan on returning it. I'm not going to break up with him over the phone. I haven't seen him since we saw each other in the airport for a couple of hours. I care about him enough to see him face to face. I did however FaceTime with Kirby late Thanksgiving night. I was honest with him and told him I had stronger feelings for one of the other guys. I could tell he was hurt and upset, even though he tried to hide it. I feel better knowing he isn't going to wait any longer for my decision. I wished him well and hoped that we could remain friends. I wouldn't blame any of these men if friendship doesn't happen. I fully understand that they only loved me while I loved them all in their own ways. It's easier for me to say let's be friends.

I have butterflies in my stomach just knowing I'm getting on a plane to find Kaiden. It has my insides turning to mush. Maybe some of it is nerves. I can't wait to get to Vegas and figure shit out with him. I am hopeful that I will find him. Mentally I am trying to prepare myself to be let down. I may not find him or he may very well tell me we aren't meant for one another.

My phone chimes to notify me I have a text. I read it real quick.

Malcolm: I am leaving California tomorrow. I

have a client I need to meet with in New York. I want to see you.

Shit! I need to think of something to say. I really don't want to break up with him over the phone.

Me: Sorry I haven't returned your calls. It's a long story that I don't want to share over the phone. How long are you going to be here? I am at the airport myself.

Malcolm: Could be a couple of weeks. Might be longer. Depends on you.

Me: What do you mean it depends on me?

Malcolm: Not something I want to discuss on text messaging. When can we have a conversation?

Me: When I get back.

Malcolm: Which is when?

Me: I may only be gone for just a couple of days.

Malcolm: Call me when you get back home.

Me: I will!

I pocket my phone after I power it off. I grab my suitcase and head toward boarding. The moment I've been waiting for is getting closer. The next five and a half hours is going to go by slowly.

I find my seat and the first thing I do is buckle up. I get out my earbuds and hit my playlist. Then I put an eye mask on and lean my head back on the headrest. I don't think about the fact that I still hate flying. I think about what I want to say to Kaiden.

❧

I feel all the air getting sucked out of my lungs. My heart beats so fast the pulse in my neck feels like it's choking me. My hope is fading fast. I left the airport and came right to Kaiden's gated home only to be told when I pressed the intercom button he doesn't own this home anymore. I didn't come here the last time I came to see him. I am running out of options to find him. The man I love has vanished and I don't know if I'll locate him. I might never see Kaiden again.

I sit in the car I rented with the engine still running. I look through the gate at the home Kaiden shared with me. The home he never shared with another woman. I think back to our first night together, me pretending to be his new hire, him showing me a glimpse of what was behind door number two, me getting attacked, then me crawling into his bed that night. I wanted so badly to not fall in love with him. We never even told each other how we felt until a couple of months later. I wish I could tell Kaiden just how much I love him right this second.

I cannot sit here and cry. Sitting here crying isn't going to help me find him. I set my maps to get me back to the strip before putting the car in reverse. I pull out onto the road and take one last look at what used to be his home. I push the feeling of loss out of my mind. I haven't lost him yet. At least until he tells me I have face to face.

I take the long drive back with the radio turned up loud. I thought by blasting the music I'd be able to tune out my thoughts. I had no such luck. My mind isn't going to stop wandering until I know that something bad didn't happen to Kaiden. The longer it is taking to find him, the more the horrible thoughts flood my mind. Was he in a car accident? Did someone hurt him while he was in his childhood neighborhood? Was he kidnapped? Did he leave the country? I try to replace the bad thoughts with good ones. The ones we shared together last April. Even better when he told me he loves me back in June.

I find a parking spot on the street. Where do I go from here? Should I get a room somewhere for the night? Should I ask Gaetano if he's heard any more gossip? Should I ask him for his help? Does he care that his brother is missing? All these questions jumble in my mind. I can't think like this.

I get out of the rental and walk to the sidewalk.

My legs start walking north on their own accord. The neon lights on the strip are beginning to light the streets as the evening rolls in. I probably shouldn't venture far. I don't need to be losing my rental car. I pass by a small cafe. My stomach reminds me I haven't eaten since breakfast. I turn back around and go inside. I'm the only customer. I order a deli sandwich and get a cup of soup to go with it. Since I'm the only one here, it doesn't take long for my food to be prepared. I take my tray to a table near the window. The girl working comes to me and gives me a cup. I forgot to order a drink. She told me to help myself to the soda fountain. That was very nice of her.

I have a few bites of my sandwich. Even though I am hungry, food isn't what I want. I glance out the window and my eyes open wide. I look around the cafè, I've been here before. I gather up my food and then dump it in the trash. I hurry outside, then step into the street without looking. My heart goes to my throat as a car's horn blares at me. I get my composure and wait for a safe time to cross. Once I cross, I don't waste a second pulling the door open to what used to be Vibe. The music isn't filling the club. The dance floor isn't jammed packed, either. I walk around scanning the area for any sign of Kaiden. Just as before, this place doesn't feel like him anymore. I take the staircase anyway to the second floor. When I reach the top, it's dark, so I go back down. I see the spiral staircase to the platform. It looks empty up there as well. I go to the bar and as I wait, I glance over to where there once was a hallway. I'm feeling defeated again. When I face the man's voice at the bar, I smile.

"Bounce, right?"

"Ms. Verbank! What brings you in here?"

"I'm actually looking for Kaiden."

"I haven't seen him in a month. Maybe even longer."

"Do you have any idea where I might find him?"

"Did you try the other club?"

"Is there another way in?"

"Oh, yes, it has its own entrance now. It's out back."

"How do I get back there?"

"There's an alley just up the block."

"Oh!"

"How about I let you out our back door."

"I'd appreciate that very much."

Bounce comes around from behind the bar. I want to ask him why he hasn't seen Kaiden in so long? Why did the name change? Why did Kaiden move?

But I don't care to get into a conversation with him. I just want to get next door to see if Kaiden is there.

Bounce opens the door. *"Good luck, Ms. Verbank."*

"Thanks."

The door slams shut on its own and I jump. It's pretty much dark and creepy out here. I look to my right and see a glass door entrance. I hurry over and pull it open. The lighting is how it used to be in the hallway, red and dim. As I take the hallway I am once again feeling like I am walking into a place I've never been. Before I reach the private club, I spin on my heels. I know he isn't here. I feel like I can't breathe. Kaiden is getting wiped out of my life as if we never met. I feel my heart breaking little by little.

CHAPTER TWO
CIARA

I don't know why I bothered checking into a hotel room. It's not like I am going to get any sleep. It is killing me not knowing where Kaiden is. It's really scaring me that I'm not going to find him. I only have one place left to go and I've already been there the last time I was here. I really don't know how to get there, either. It's always been dark when I've gone. The first time, I fell asleep and the second time Gaetano drove me and I was pretty upset. I cannot ask him to take me back. I do remember I saw a street sign that read Forest St. just before the car slowed. If that's not the right street, I might at least get closer than I am sitting here in a hotel room.

I grab my cell phone and open the maps, typing in Forest Street. I look at the first one that comes up. It's only a half hour drive. I know it's much further than that. I look at the second one and tap on it to read the directions. I think about it for a minute or two. Fuck it! I'm going. I won't get any rest without knowing I at least tried.

I grab the keys to the rental off the table along with my room key card, and my purse. I get my jacket on my way out of the room, putting it on as I take the hallway to the elevators. Once I am inside, I remember Kaiden and I stayed in a hotel after we left his moms. I google Taylor Knights hotel. I smile when I see it's only a twenty minute difference between Forest St. and the hotel. I might just get lucky and find Kaiden's childhood home all on my own. I cross my fingers that I find him, as well. My hopes are lifted slightly.

꙳

After the two hour drive, I am on Forest Street. It's dark and spooky. I drive slowly, looking for the house. My stomach is in knots. What am I going to do if I can't find the house? I didn't think about that part before I took off in the late evening hours. It's almost eleven. I am not driving all the way back to Vegas. I might not have a choice, though, all of my stuff is there. I should have brought it with me. If Kaiden isn't here, I'm out of options. I'll have to give up. I'll have nothing left to do besides go back to my life alone.

I slam on the brakes as a stray cat runs out in front of me. I catch my breath before I let off on the brake. I let the car coast forward at a snail's pace as I kept looking for the house. As I pass one place, it looks like it. I back up and pull to the side of the street. I throw the car in park, turn off the engine, and get out. I found it! Just like the last time I was here, there's one light on inside. I hear a noise behind me, I hit the lock button on the rental as I run for the weathered front porch. I say a prayer, *"Please be here,"* before I knock. I wait for a minute before I open the door. My heart skips a few beats when I peek my head inside. I walk in on shaky legs. Tears fill my eyes as I stand here and stare. My beautiful man is sitting in a half beat up chair, sleeping. I take a few deep breaths before I tiptoe over to him. I get down to his level and reach out a hand, touching his beard that is no longer kept short. As my fingers comb through it, he doesn't even stir. I lean in and put my lips to his, kissing him lightly. His eyes blink open and he gives me a dead stare. I pull back a little.

"Tell me I'm not dreaming," he says in a raspy voice.

CHAPTER 2

"You aren't dreaming." He jumps from the ratty chair, startling me. *"Kaiden?"*

"I've waited a long time for you to come back. Why are you here now?"

My heart sinks. He doesn't want me here. I stand. *"I came sooner, but you weren't here."*

"What do you mean you came sooner here? As in here, here?" He asks, pointing to the floor.

"Yes here! After I went to what used to be Vibe, I came here. I saw this place and thought you didn't wait for me. I left. I went home."

"Why are you back now?"

He seems angry. My fears are coming true. He didn't want to be found. Kaiden was running from me.

"I love you, you idiot," I spit out with an attitude.

I head for the door. I don't need the third degree from him to know he doesn't love me. I get the door slightly opened to have it slammed back shut. His body is so close to mine. His mouth is near my ear.

"Say it again."

"I love you."

"I love you so fucking much, Ciara."

"Why haven't you returned my calls?"

"I dropped a hammer on my phone the day before Thanksgiving. I haven't cared to get a new one. I

figured it was over. November ended and you didn't come."

"But I did come. I wanted to surprise you and I'm the one who was surprised. What happened to you?"

Kaiden turns me to face him. *"Ciara, I waited the entire month for you at my home. You never went there. If I had known you'd come looking for me here, I would have been here waiting for you."*

I put my head down. *"I'm such an idiot. I should have called you."*

"Look at me. You're here now, right?"

"Yes."

"Are you here to stay?" I shake my head yes. *"Then that's all that matters to me."*

I get up on my tiptoes, putting both my arms around his neck. I put my mouth to his and I kiss him with everything I have. I love this man so much. I don't ever want to be away from him ever again. I have so much to share with him, but right now I just want to stay where we are.

CHAPTER THREE
KAIDEN

Opening my eyes and seeing Ciara was surprising to say the least. I have waited months to have her come to my home and tell me she chose me. I dreamed of sweeping her into my arms and holding onto her so tight that she could never leave me again for many, many nights. Ciara Verbank has done something nobody else has been capable of doing. She got me to fall so hard and deeply in love with her. There is no doubt in my mind that I'll love her till the day I die. I want her to be my wife, the mother of my children, and so much more. She's it for me. When she told me she loved me, I needed to hear it again. I want to hear it every day until my time on earth is done.

I'm sure we have so much to discuss, but I want to stay in this moment with her. Having Ciara in my embrace, her lips on mine, her body this damn close,

I'm not ready to let her go just yet. We have months to make up for. I kiss her delicate neck.

"I was terrified I wasn't going to find you."

"I was terrified you'd never choose me."

Ciara slips out of my grip. She walks away, while removing her jacket. I keep my eyes on her as she spins around to face me. She takes the hem of her sweater and starts to lift it. I walk over and stop her. Her eyes squint as she can't believe I am stopping her.

"You don't want me?"

"Baby, I want you, never doubt that. Look around, this isn't the place. I have a room at Taylor Knights, let's go there."

"If you hadn't fallen asleep, you would not have been here, am I right?"

"That's a possibility. Let's not focus on that. We are together and that is all the matters."

"You are right."

I pick up her jacket and help her into it. Then grab my jacket off the floor as well and put it on.

"Did you drive here?"

"I did."

"We'll put it in the garage for the night and take mine."

"Are you sure that's safe?"

CHAPTER 3

"Safer than being on the street."

I take her hand and kiss the back. *"Ready?"*

She nods her head. I keep hold of her hand as we leave and go out to the garage. I open her door on the passenger side for her to get in. I can't believe she came here not once, but twice. I've told her before this isn't a very safe neighborhood. I'd never allow her to come here alone. It won't be happening again. I get in and drive my vehicle out, then off to the side. I hold my hand out for her to give me the keys to the rental. I get out and walk to the street where she parked. It gives me chills knowing the woman I love came here. This is no place for a woman to be alone, especially in such a nice car. I always hated my mother coming and going in the dark. She did a lot of walking back then. I hate myself for ever leaving her here. I should have gotten her out of here when I left. I'll never forgive myself for letting her pass away in such a horrible place.

I get in the car and I'm relieved I'm getting Ciara out of here. *"Promise me no matter what happens that you'll never ever come back to this place alone."*

"I promise. If it makes you feel better, I wasn't alone the first time."

"What do you mean you weren't alone?"

"Gaetano brought me when I asked him to."

That doesn't make me feel any better at all. My brother is a pompous ass and I'd love for him to stay the hell away from my woman. I don't trust Gaetano or my asshole, sperm donor, father. Both of them can just stay the fuck out of my life. I want nothing to do with either of them. Ciara has no idea what a snake in the grass they both really are.

I shove that anger away. I have Ciara back and I'm not going to let anger for them overtake this moment. I have everything I need in life sitting right next to me. Nothing is going to spoil this happiness I'm feeling.

"I wish I had brought my suitcase."

"We can go back and get it."

"It's not in the car. I have a room on the strip."

"Where at? I can have it brought to us." I really hope she doesn't say Seven Jewels.

"Diamond Palace."

Relief once again washes over me tonight. *"Good, I know the owner. Your stuff will be at the hotel by morning."*

A few minutes later I turned into the parking lot of Taylor Knights. Ciara won't be needing any clothes tonight anyway. She already has too many on as it is. Stopping her from stripping back at my mom's wasn't easy. I wasn't about to have my way with her body in a pile of dust. But now that we are in my room, I'm going to ravish every single inch of her. I'm not going to leave any part of her untouched. I am going to make Ciara mine all over again. No man will ever put their hands on her body again unless it's me.

"This is the same room we had when you brought me here."

"It is."

I help her out of her jacket and hang it in the closet. I do the same with mine. She takes in the room the same way she did the first time we were here. The only difference is I have a few of my things here.

"Are you living here?"

"Staying, not living."

"What's the difference?"

I bring her to me. *"Do you really want to discuss my living arrangements right now or would you rather I help you out of these clothes?"*

"Talking is overrated."

I lift her sweater, my knuckles lightly graze her flesh. I've missed the sound of her breath hitching when I touch her. I brush her hair over her shoulder as I bend and put my mouth to her neck. Her perfume fills my senses and my body reacts instantly. I reach around to her back to unhook her bra. My hands feel her upper body beneath my palms as I slip them to her front. My fingertips feel her erect nipples as my hands cup her breasts. Ciara tugs on my shirt. I use one hand to pull it over my head. When I bring her back in close, our upper bodies are skin on skin. Having my girl pressed against me is a feeling I never want to lose. The thoughts that ran through my mind in the eight long, torturous months she was gone, I never want to experience them ever again. I felt the life getting sucked out of me every month that passed by without her. The only thing that kept me going was hope. Hope that she'd come back to me.

I open her jeans and tug them down past her hips. I kiss her navel as I work them off her legs. I glance up at her beautiful face that I've missed so very much. I run my fingers ever so lightly up the backs of her legs. All the way up over her ass and to the top of her little lace panties. I then slide my fingers into the waistband and drag them down and off her body. Getting to my feet, I kiss her before I lift her into my arms, carrying her to the bed. Removing my own jeans, my eyes take in every delicious inch of her. Once my own clothing is removed, I get on the bed next to her. I cover us with the comforter and bring her to my body. Having her snuggled up next to me, is complete happiness. When her hand begins to explore, I take her hand and lace our fingers together.

"Is something wrong?" she asks.

"Nothing is wrong. Everything is finally right. I just want to hold you in my arms and feel your body next to mine skin to skin."

Ciara tilts her head to look at me. *"I never want to move. I want to stay like this forever."*

Silence falls between us. I run my fingers along her back. I feel her body relax into mine. It's so quiet I can hear my own heartbeat mixed with hers. I like this sound. Peace has finally settled my mind.

CHAPTER FOUR
CIARA

About an hour or so ago I woke up next to an amazing man. I laid next to him and watched him sleep. The longer I watched him sleep the more I knew why this amazing man captured my heart. My heart is full of happiness just knowing this man is back in my life. I don't ever want to be separated from Kaiden ever again. I can't really explain to anyone how I came to this decision that he's the one. I sat at the Thanksgiving dinner table with family and he's the one that I wished was there the most. He's the one I missed. Kaiden is the one I couldn't picture celebrating another holiday without. This man just does something to me that I can't put into words.

I leaned over top of Kaiden and kissed his cheek. His eyes never opened and his breathing didn't change. His arm came around my shoulders, though, so I then settled back up against him. I closed my eyes and hugged him. I must have fallen back to sleep because the next time I opened my eyes, I was alone in the king size bed. The bathroom door was left slightly opened and I could hear the shower running. Once I pulled the covers back to get out of bed, I grabbed the bathrobe that was left at the foot of the bed for me. I heard the shower shutting off as I reached the ajared door. I'm a little disappointed I missed showering with him, but I open it the rest of the way anyway. My heart turns to mush as soon as I lay my eyes on him.

"Good morning," he says.

"Good morning."

He gives me the bathroom after he kisses me. I do my thing and then brush my teeth. Kaiden comes back and stands beside me, his fingers comb through his hair. I watch as he looks at himself in the mirror, then reaches for his clippers. I sit on the bathroom vanity when he begins to trim his beard.

"Did you sell your home?"

"I did."

"Why?"

"I put it on the market after I saw you in June."

"Okay, but why did you do that?"

"I didn't want you to feel obligated to move to Vegas when you came back to me."

"What about Vibe? Did you just change the name after the renovation?"

"I sold that too."

"I would never want you to change your life or who you are to be with me."

Kaiden finishes trimming his beard then sets the clippers down. *"Vegas isn't you. It's not home to you."*

"But it is to you."

He puts his hands on the countertop on both sides of me. He leans down to my level. *"Not really. At least not anymore. I feel I have outgrown my stay here. I'm ready for a new adventure with you."*

"What about the real Vibe?"

"That's still ours."

I smiled when he called it ours. I feel the bathrobe strap untying then getting pulled out from the two loops. The robe falls open, exposing my naked body to the man I love. Both of Kaiden's hands go to the inside of the robe, holding onto my waist, he pulls me closer to the edge of the counter. I reach for the towel still wrapped around his waist and drop it to the floor. Kaiden rests his forehead to mine.

CHAPTER 4

"I want nothing more than to ravish your body right now, but I have to get back to my mom's."

"Can't it wait?"

"It can't, I have people stopping by. I have to be there. I'd love it if you came with me."

"I do have to get the rental back." I reach up and run my fingers through his trimmed beard. *"I like this much better."*

He puts his hands to my shoulders and slips the bathrobe off. *"I like this much better. I wish I could cancel the appointments."* He kisses me. *"We better get dressed before I change my mind and be a no show."*

"I wouldn't object to that."

"I know." He kisses me again before leaving the bathroom.

I bite my bottom lip. I am just so goddamn happy. Sex would be nice, but nothing beats just being with him.

🍂

We reach Kaiden's mom's old house and there are a few vehicles parked alongside the road. I read the business names on the sides. I'm a little confused by what's going on. These are construction companies. If Vegas isn't home, why are these people here?

We get out and Kaiden shakes hands with the men, then we all go inside. While they roll blueprints out to look them over, I pick a picture up off the floor. It's a photo of Ms. Marcellus. She's wearing a ball gown. It's absolutely beautiful. I shove the picture inside my jacket pocket.

"Ms. Verbank is a designer." I hear Kaiden tell one guy. *"Ciara, what do you think of these blueprints?"*

I put my attention on the rolled out paper. My eyes then travel over the space. *"When you have guests over they would have to go through either the master bedroom or one of the two bedrooms to use the restroom."*

"Good point."

The man hooves over the paper. He points to an area. *"We can add a half bathroom here if we cut out some of the dining room space."*

"Nah, I don't like that idea. There has to be another way."

I speak up. *"Why can't you add another floor? Move the bedrooms to a second floor."*

"I love it. Brilliant idea, babe."

CHAPTER 4

I smile, even though I still have no idea why I am. Is he doing this for us?

"I'll need more time to draw out new blueprints. What will go where the bedrooms were?"

"Just make the rooms bigger down here and make sure there is a usable bathroom. Take the way the bedrooms are set up now but move them to an upstairs."

The guy points to the paper. *"I'll add a staircase here. Master bedroom on the left and the two others on the right."*

"Perfect. How long should all this take?"

"A couple weeks if the weather holds out a few more days."

"Sounds wonderful. I am aiming to have this place done by Christmas Eve."

"I'll do my best. I brought catalogs for style options. I'll need to know what you want as soon as possible if we are going to get this done on time."

"Ciara and I will let you know what we want by the end of the day."

"I'm done. My boys can start the tear off today and I need to order more materials. Should be able to start the rebuild as of tomorrow."

"Thank you, Hank."

"My pleasure."

Kaiden asks if I'm ready to go. He gets the catalogs and then gets my rental out of the garage. We decided to meet back at the hotel. I'm still clueless about what's really going on with that house. It doesn't make sense to me if he's renovating it for us after he made me promise to never come here again without him.

CHAPTER FIVE
KAIDEN

Last night was the best I slept in months. Having Ciara back in my arms is almost unbelievable. To wake up this morning to find it all wasn't a dream was exciting, thrilling, and heartwarming. All hope was restored. I'm not going to lie, there's a part of me waiting to see if this is real. The question remains in the back of my mind, am I going to wake up tomorrow or the next day to have her tell me she made a mistake? I sure hope not. I can't lose Ciara again. It would destroy me. I don't believe she knows just how madly in love with her that I truly am. I plan on showing her every day we are together. I need to shove this little bit of doubt out of my mind. I also need to not think about the other men she had a relationship with.

Ciara parks her rental right next to me. Just seeing her this close is mind-blowing. Once November passed and I didn't see her, I thought I had lost her for good. I hated how that made me feel. I couldn't sleep, I barely ate, and I didn't care about my future. I was just letting the days get away from me. My beard showed how much I didn't care about anything. I feel life coming back.

"Are you hungry?"

"Yes, very."

"How about we grab a bite to eat while we look through those catalogs Hank gave us?"

"As long as you are feeding me, we can do whatever you want."

"Hmm, maybe we should order in."

"If that is what you want."

"Tempting! There's a diner not far from here. If we stay here, we'll never get to looking at countertops, cabinets, and other things that we need to pick out."

We get in my SUV and I reach over to hold her hand as I drive. The diner is only a couple of blocks, so all too soon her hand is gone. I hold the door open for her as we enter. I see one booth open. Lucky for us it's tucked away in a corner. We sit beside each other and read the same menu. Ciara hardly looked over the menu before she announced that she is getting the cheeseburger club and French fries. I put the menu back where I got it from. I am getting the same as her. It isn't until after we place our order that we begin to talk.

"Kaiden, I'm confused about what is going on with your mom's old house."

"I went for a drive one night last month and ended up at my mom's. I was looking through photos and I started to feel guilty. Out of frustration, I then started knocking down the walls. After I was done, I figured it was a good time to let go of the past. I have a buddy from back in my school days that went to prison three years ago for something he didn't do. He's getting out on Christmas day. He had a newborn when he got convicted. Sam wants to start his life over. With no job, no place to really go, I want to help him. He needs time to reconnect to his wife and daughter without worry. So, I am giving the house a makeover for them."

"You are giving them your house?"

"I am. It's time for me to move on. I think I've kept the house all this time to punish myself. Guilt eats me alive every day as it is. Going there makes it worse."

Ciara wraps her arms around me. *"You have nothing to feel guilty about."*

"I do. I could have gotten her out of that place. If I had she wouldn't have died alone."

"Kaiden, that isn't your fault. You have to ask yourself if she would have left if she had a chance."

"She probably wouldn't have. I still should have tried."

"You need to stop beating yourself up for it. You need to remember the good times the two of you had. Now, because of you another family will get to be a family in that place and that is remarkable. Your mom would be proud of you and what you have accomplished."

Ciara turns my head and kisses me.

"She'd like you."

"I'm sure I would have liked her."

"Want to help me pick things out for the house?"

"I do!"

🐾

We sat at the diner combing through the catalogs for hours. Even though we weren't picking out things for our own home, it felt like we were. Some day we will be doing this for us and that is inspiring. Every minute that passes, I feel us getting

CHAPTER 5

closer. I know we still have a lot to discuss, but doing this together is a move in the right direction. I am truly starting to believe Ciara is really mine. My negative thoughts are slipping further into the back of my mind.

After we dropped off the choices we made to the contractor, we came back to the hotel. I want nothing more in this moment than to feel her body pressed against mine with no clothing between us. Before I make her mine again, I have questions that I need answers to. But before I can do that, I need to find out why my girl has gone quiet. She is lost in thought, if I know her the way I think I do, she is worried about something.

I climb up on the bed next to her. *"What are you thinking about? You've been quiet ever since we left the house."*

"You know I love you, and want to be with you, right?"

"That's what I'm hoping for since you showed up here."

"So you don't know that?" She crawls over my lap and sits on top of me. She takes my face in her hands. *"I want us. I love you more than words could ever express."*

"You have that stress line in your forehead you get

when tension takes over. What are you worried about?"

"I have to go back home."

"So, we will go to New York. When do we need to go?"

"As soon as possible."

I sit up straighter and kiss her. *"I have nothing here anymore to tie me to this place. It's why I sold everything. Whatever Hank needs from me from here on forward can be done by phone."*

"Umm."

"You do want me to go with you, right?"

"I haven't broken up with Malcolm, yet."

"I see."

"I haven't been able to see him in person and I didn't want to do it over the phone. He's been very kind to me and respectful. I want to return that respect. I don't want you to doubt that I'll change my mind because I won't. I love you and I can't imagine being without you."

"Did you love him?"

"I did. The thing is, my love for you is stronger and I know in my heart that you are the one I want to be with."

I hate knowing she loved another man. It bothers me more than I want it to. I should just be happy knowing she chose me in this fucked up situation. I could kick myself in my own ass knowing I should have asked her out the first time I ever saw her. I wouldn't be feeling this jealousy I feel if I had. I never experienced jealousy until I met her. It's an ugly feeling. I don't like it one bit.

"What do you want me to do?"

"I want you to come with me. Before we can begin to build our future, I need to do this one last thing."

"Then let's book our flight to New York."

"Really!?"

"Ciara, I just got you back. No way am I going to be separated from you this soon."

"I want to show you how serious I am about us."

I put my lips to her neck and taste her delicate skin. *"How do you suggest to do that, Ms. Verbank?"* I say between kisses.

"I want you to take me to Vibe tonight. I want to experience whatever you held back on before."

I inch my mouth up to her ear. *"Are you sure about that? If we do this, I'm not letting you go. You will be mine."*

"I want to be yours and only yours."

I scoot us to the edge of the bed and stand, then set her back on the mattress. *"I'm going to book us the first tickets out of here to New York."*

Ciara is going to be disappointed, but I am not taking her to Vibe tonight. I'll save that for another time. I need to get her back home. She has a man dangling in the wind and until he's gone, I can't do everything I want to do.

CHAPTER SIX
CIARA

Reuniting with Kaiden has been odd at times. Picking out household things together was inspiring. Our future feels it is heading in the right direction. Although every minute we've been together has been wonderful, I can't help but feel he's holding back a little. I asked him to take me to Vibe and he didn't take advantage of that. I'm not upset, I'm more worried as to why he wouldn't take me there. I am giving myself to Kaiden willingly. I am ready to learn more about the world he lived in before we met. Kaiden and I have experienced his sexual preference, but I know he only showed me a tiny bit of what that really consists of. I don't want Kaiden to feel he has to give up who he is to be with me. He already sold his club, his home, and is about to give his mom's place away. I don't want him to change at all. I love the man just the way he is.

"You have the same expression you had earlier today. What is troubling your mind?"

"Why didn't you take me to Vibe? We had enough time before we got on this plane."

"It wasn't the right time."

"You get I broke up with nine other men to be with you, right? You know I am giving myself to you, correct?"

"Of course I know that. Technically you have broken up with eight guys. Until you cut ties with Malcolm you aren't completely mine."

"You think I'm going to change my mind, don't you?"

"No, I don't think that at all. Ciara, you were mine for a month. You were theirs for a month. You are not mine completely until you are no longer one of theirs. Does that make sense?"

"I think so." I look down toward my lap and pick at the threads that hang loosely from the rip in my jeans. *"You sold your home and your club because you say Vegas isn't home for me. You did that to prove how much you want to be with me. Why do I feel you are holding back?"*

"Ciara, sweetheart, look at me." I pick my head up and look him in the eyes. *"You are the only person I have ever fallen in love with. This is new to me. I*

don't do relationships and I don't want to fuck anything up between us. I have never experienced this little bit of jealousy I'm feeling inside."

"Jealousy... of what?"

"That you fell in love with other men while I waited all these months to see if what we had is real. A little part of me is wishing love wasn't what you felt for anyone but me."

Kaiden wipes the tear that fell to my cheek. *"You have nothing to be jealous about. What I felt for any of the other men doesn't compare to how I feel about you. How can I prove that to you?"*

"Tell me why you love me over everyone else."

I am taken back by his question. *"What happened to you in the last six months?"*

"What?"

"One of the reasons I love you is because you are confident, strong minded, and a dominant man. You take what you want and don't hold back."

Kaiden leans over and kisses me with such passion that my heart melts. I'm scared that my dating other men is going to ruin us.

"I'm still that man. I just need you to break up with Malcolm."

"I plan on doing that as soon as I can see him."

"I know."

Coming back to Kaiden hasn't been as easy as I thought it would be. I don't know what I expected, I guess. Him opening his arms and not caring I was with other men? Pick up where we left off as if we didn't just spend six months apart? I can't help but feel that I need to prove my love for him is real. He has to know I chose him because I want our lives together and our love to grow stronger. I'll prove that to him somehow.

❦

The moment we get to Grams', my smile is big. The tree is arriving at the same time we are. I love this time of year. The smell of pine fills the family room. The Christmas lights give off a warm glow. When you go out, people's homes are all decked out. Then there's the cookies, hot cocoa, and a warm fireplace.

"That is one large tree," Kaiden says.

"I know! Don't you just love it!?"

"Ya, I guess."

"Kaiden, don't tell me you are one of those people who dislike Christmas!"

"I liked it when I was very, very little. By the time I was ten-ish I wasn't too thrilled about it anymore."

"I hope I can make you love it all over again."

He brings me to him and kisses my forehead. *"I think you are off to a good start."*

"Are you ready to face Grams?"

"Of course!"

We get inside and Grams is bossing the tree guy around. I laugh. I don't think Kaiden knows what he's walking into. The tree in the foyer is just for show. There will be one in the family room and the sunroom as well. Grams goes all out when it comes to decorating for Christmas. I'm sure tomorrow she'll have the crew here to do the outdoor lights.

"Kinda late in the night to be getting a tree delivery."

Grams turns around and her smile is radiating. It's not me she is smiling at. It's Kaiden. She comes toward us with her arms held out wide open. I'm actually surprised she hugs me first after the smile she gave to my boyfriend.

"Welcome home, dear."

"Thanks! I love the tree!"

She stands back and looks me over before letting her arms drop. I haven't told her Kaiden is the one I want to be with. I bet she's wondering if he's the one or if I'm still making up my mind. She steps over to Kaiden and then hugs him. *"Welcome."*

"Thank you, Millie. I'm happy to be here."

"I have to finish up with these guys. While I'm doing that how about you kids get settled in and freshen up. Katie is in the kitchen baking some cookies. Join me for tea in about a half-hour?"

"We'd love that," Kaiden says.

I look at the eight-foot tree. I can't wait to get the boxes of ornaments out. It's one of my favorite parts of the holiday. Going through the box, picking the right ones, and remembering when Grams or I gave it to each other. Kaiden put his arm around my waist and whispered in my ear. I take his hand and begin to take him up the grand staircase. I am already thinking about how I am going to make this the best Christmas he's ever had.

We get to my room and Kaiden shuts the door behind us. He comes up from behind me as I put my suitcase by the dresser. His hands come to my front and he starts to take my jacket off. I inhale a breath.

"I have a feeling you think I don't want you. I want you, Ciara. There should be no doubt about that in your mind. I'm going to take care of any doubt you may have."

His hands slip underneath my sweater. The warmth of his hands mixed with the chill from the loss of my jacket makes my body react in a sensual way. I desperately want Kaiden to strip me from my clothing and make love to me. I want us to reconnect the sexual chemistry we both feel for one another. If we did, it might help us get back to where we left off. I lean back against his strong manly frame and turn my head. My eyes close, my lips part as he cups my breasts. I fall deeper under his spell he has on me.

"You have too many clothes on. You should take them off for me."

All too soon the warmth of his hands is gone. I know the only way for him to touch me again is to do what he asks, so I turn to face him. Lifting my sweater, I remove it. Then I move to my jeans and take them off. I am left standing in front of Kaiden in just my bra and panties. The last time I got naked for him, we didn't have sex. Which was fine. I loved every second of being in his arms, skin on skin. I need him this time. There is nothing I want more than to feel him inside of me.

Kaiden strips from his pullover shirt. I eagerly wait for him to remove the rest of his clothes. *"I believe you still have too many clothes on, Ms. Verbank."*

I bite my bottom lip as he takes his jeans off. For a moment I can't believe I get to spend the rest of my life with this gorgeous man. He's all mine. I get to be with Kaiden in ways nobody else gets to ever again.

I yelp when I am pulled to his body. He lifts me slightly off the floor and carries me across the room. After he sets me down, he sits on the foot of the bed, leaving me standing between his legs. Suddenly I am bent over his lap before I can blink. His hand comes down on my ass. I want more. I smile when he spanks me again for not listening to his command. That smile fades the harder the contact is with each smack. By the time he stops my body wants the pleasure that comes with the sting that is left on my bottom more than ever. Even more so when his fingers slip beneath my panties, teasing the flesh of my ass. Just as before, his touch is gone too soon.

"Stand," he says with a firm voice.

I don't know how but I manage to get to my feet. I am only facing him for a split second before he spins my body. I gasp when I hear the tearing of my panties. He runs his palms over my butt, then up my back. I look over my shoulder as he unhooks my bra. He turns me to face him once again. His eyes comb over my nakedness.

"Your body is mine, Ciara. Mine to please, to ravish, and to control. Next time I tell you to bare

yourself to me, that is what I want you to do. Understood?"

"Yes."

"I don't need Vibe to show you all of me. I just needed your willingness and permission to explore my lifestyle fully."

"I want all of you, Kaiden, even what I don't know already. I am willing, I just need to know what you want me to do."

"You'll learn, all in good time. Right now I want to give you what you desire. What I desire."

Kaiden brings me closer to him and I straddle his lap, taking him inside me. I rock my hips back and forth, feeling every inch of him filling me to the core. I use his body for my pleasure. For his pleasure. I fall deeper in love with him as our bodies become reacquainted. Kaiden is the only man I ever want to please me, to cherish me, and to love me. I know in this moment that we are two damaged souls that are healed when we are one.

CHAPTER SEVEN
KAIDEN

I told Ciara I'd meet her in the kitchen for a muffin that she brags about after I make a few phone calls. Last night I received a call from the contractor working on my mom's house. I didn't answer it because I was in the company of two beautiful women who had my full attention. Listening to Ciara and Millie interact with one another brought back memories of conversations I once had with my mother. These two are close as my mom and I once were. Long before I set off to make a name for myself in Vegas. Knowing Ciara and Millie are as close as I thought is heartwarming. I'm happy to see that Millie truly does want the best for Ciara.

Once I am done with my calls, I make my way to the first level. I hear a loud screech from what I believe to be the family room. I pick up my pace. I know that is Ciara. I enter the room and see my girl holding an oversized stuffed teddy bear with a Santa hat on. I stand back, pushing the mini heart attack I just had out of my mind and watch my girl. She sets the teddy bear off to the side and begins digging through a tote. Her joy for Christmas shines through her beauty. I move into the room more to get a closer look. She holds up an ornament that she clearly must have made as a kid. I think back to all the times I brought home one for my mom from school. Our Christmas trees were nothing like the Verbank's trees. Mine and moms were so small it only took one strand of lights and the only ornaments were the ones I had made. Seeing Ciara still having hers, I wish I had mine. Not because I made them, but for the purpose of remembering the smile I put on my mom's face.

I feel a touch on my upper arm. *"She's beautiful, isn't she?"*

"Extremely!"

"May I have a word with you in private?"

"I promised Ciara I'd have breakfast with her."

"Come find me in my office when she leaves."

She's leaving? Where is she going? She didn't tell me she had anything to do today.

"I will find you."

Millie nods her head, she looks at Ciara one last time before leaving the family room. I take a few more moments just watching Ciara in her glory of Christmas magic before I walk over to where she is on the floor. When I reach her, I crouch down to her level. She has her nose buried in the tote, so I take her by surprise. I reach out and take hold of her face before leaning in and planting my lips on hers. Her mouth curls up at the corners when our lips part.

"A little birdie told me that there are these really amazing muffins waiting for us to devour in the kitchen."

"Oh, smart birdie you have in your ear."

I stand and hold out my hand to help her up. Once she's to her feet, I bend to pick up the ornament she was admiring minutes ago. *"How old were you when you made this one?"*

"I don't remember."

"I made one sorta like this one when I was about eight. I have to admit, yours is much prettier."

"I bet yours was remarkable and your mom probably loved it."

"She did." I take her hand. *"I can't wait to see the smile it brings to your face when our kids bring home stuff like this to you."*

Ciara touches my cheek. *"You mean to us."*

"Let's go eat."

We leave the family room. Ciara and I haven't talked about kids much, so I'm not sure where that thought came from. I'm not even sure I want any children. If we do decide to have them, it won't be for a few years. I'm selfishly not ready to share her with anyone.

Ciara gets a blueberry muffin for herself and a banana nut one for me. She has her tea with hers and I have coffee. I take the first bite as she looks on. I moan. She is right, they are excellent muffins. One might not be satisfying. I may need two.

"Oh shit! I didn't realize how much time had passed. I am going to be late if I don't get a move on it."

"Late to where?"

"I called Malcolm. I am meeting him at my store."

"Want me to come with you?"

"Sorry, but no. I need to do this on my own."

"I understand. I'm sure I can find something to do while you're gone."

Ciara gets up and kisses my cheek. *"I love you."*

"I love you, too."

On one hand I don't like that she's going off to see one of the men she dated. On the other I'm glad she's officially ending it with Malcolm. It will be a relief to me and a load off her shoulders. A big step forward in our relationship.

I finish off my muffin and coffee before I go searching in this mansion for Millie. This home is incredibly too big for two people. It's beautiful nonetheless just too damn big. It shouldn't take me fifteen minutes to find her office.

I knock on the door. *"Hello."*

"Ahh, Kaiden, come on in and have a seat."

"You wanted a word with me."

"I did. Has Ciara left?"

"Yes, a little bit ago."

"Does Ciara know you are the one that got Ciaro and his family to come here for Thanksgiving?"

"Not unless you or he told her."

"How did you find out he's her father?"

"I got it from the source's mouth as did someone else. I didn't know that until I saw Ciaro, though. I guess I missed Ciara by just a few hours."

"So you are the one that has captured my granddaughter's heart! Ciaro told me after you found out Ciara knew about him that you asked for her hand in marriage."

"How do you feel about that?"

"If you and Ciara are madly in love, I couldn't be more thrilled. It's very honorable, Kaiden."

"So this isn't about disapproval?"

"No, Kaiden dear, I wouldn't have asked you to bid on Ciara if I already didn't approve of you."

"I'm happy you said that. Just so you know, it wouldn't have mattered to me if you didn't approve. I wouldn't have left Ciara."

"Good she picked a man who doesn't let anyone stand in his way. I asked to speak with you because I have a serious question for you."

"I'm all ears."

"I have known you for a very long time. I'm going to be very blunt with you, as you would be with me." I nod my head for her to continue. *"Do you plan on asking Ciara to marry you?"*

"I do when the time is right. That could be today, tomorrow, or months from now."

"So a December wedding may not happen?"

"It may not. There's always another December next year. I don't see what the rush is."

"When I put all this together I never really thought there'd be a wedding this month. I said that to show how serious I was. Now things have changed. I want what I originally said."

"I can only think of one reason why you'd want that. Are you ill, Millie?"

"No, I am not ill. I'm in good health."

"Then why?"

"I'm going to let you in on a secret."

I sit here and let everything sink in about what Millie just told me, I feel the pressure on my shoulders building to marry Ciara. I want to marry her, I just didn't want to rush into a wedding. Ciara deserves to have the wedding of her dreams. Cramming all the planning it takes into a few short weeks doesn't sound like a dream wedding if you ask me. I have to seriously think about this and figure out if this is the right thing to do. I don't like that Millie put this secret in my hands. It's not fair to me or Ciara.

I stand. *"I'll let you know what I decide."*

"Please do. I have the invitations ready to be mailed out. Before you say anything, Ciara picked out the invitations back in June."

As much as that statement peaks my curiosity, I need air. I am not used to someone basically telling me what I should do with my life. It's not only my life I need to make decisions for.

CHAPTER EIGHT
CIARA

Walking into my store surprises Porter. I thought he was going to climb over the counter to get to me. He actually might have if there weren't customers in the store. He quickly recovered his excitement and casually came around the counter to hug me. It feels good to hug my best friend. It's been a few days since we talked. Last he knew I was still in Vegas looking for Kaiden.

"You are glowing! I take it you found your man?"

"I did."

"It must be as amazing as you thought."

"It is. I mean we've had a few odd times, but, Porter, I truly found the person I want to spend the rest of my life with."

"Baby girl, I'm so happy for you."

My attention goes to the door when it opens. My stomach does flip flops. I so don't want to face Malcolm.

I want to see him, however, I'm about to hurt him and I am not happy about that. This isn't going to be easy. I know I have to do this, I just wish I didn't have to.

"Thank you."

"What's going on?"

"Malcolm is on his way here."

"Oh boy!"

"Yeah, I hate this."

"If you can get through breaking up with Wyatt, you can get through this one. I know Wyatt and Malcolm meant a great deal to you. You made your decision and you have to stick with it. Just remember you have Kaiden when all is said and done."

"I know, it is the only thing giving me the courage to get this done with."

The door opens again and this time nobody is leaving, Malcolm is coming in.

"I'll be right here if you need me."

Malcolm comes right to me and reaches out for a hug. I hug him. He places a kiss on top of my head. I feel so goddamn guilty. I grab his hand and drag him to the back room. I can't let this stretch out or I'm going to burst into tears before I get a word out.

I take one look at him in the eyes and it's too late. The tears build behind my lids.

"Hey," he says, pulling me into his embrace. *"what's wrong?"*

"I'm sorry, Malcolm, I love someone else." I had no intention of blurting that out like that.

He holds me tighter for a moment longer before he tells me to have a seat. He pulls the spare chair over to where I am. I want to pull my hands away when he takes hold of them.

"I knew once I was the first guy that this would be a long shot for me to get the girl. I have no regrets, Ciara. I'll always be grateful that I was lucky enough to spend time with such an amazing person. You showed me the kind of woman I want to be with. I'll settle for nothing less."

"I care about you very deeply. I hope you know that."

"I do. I know you didn't fake feelings for me."

"You are a fantastic man, Malcolm, and I hope you find someone to love. You deserve it."

"I wish I knew what difference it would have made between us if we dated later instead of eleven months ago."

I don't have the guts to tell him that when I looked back on our relationship it felt like he was more of the big brother I never had. That's just cruel.

He doesn't need to know that. Instead I tell him the truth.

"Honestly, it probably wouldn't have mattered. I know that sounds mean, but I love Kaiden and I can't change that."

"Was he one of the last?"

"No, he was actually the fourth guy."

"I see."

"I don't like this. I don't like hurting you."

"I know. I am hurt, but I don't blame you for following your heart. I have nothing but happy thoughts for your future."

"You know we can still be friends if you'd like."

"I'd like that very much." Malcolm kisses the back of my hand, then stands. *"I better get going."* He drops my hands and nods his head for his goodbye.

Just like that he's gone. I feel sick to my stomach. I didn't like that one bit. Malcolm was hurt deeply. Deeper than he'd admit. I'll be surprised if we remain friends. I can only hope that we do because I genuinely like him.

🐝

I couldn't just shove what I had to do away and pretend it didn't happen. I took some time to get over hurting someone I care about, so I stayed in my store to get it looking more festive. I thought that Porter would have started to decorate my store for Christmas in my absence, but he hasn't. What a great way to clear my mind and get my focus back on mine and Kaiden's relationship. I was putting one of those lighted white deer in the display window when I had a thought. Apparently I had no idea how long I've been lost in thought. I didn't even hear the bell ring on the door when it opened.

"I've been watching you stare out the window for a while now trying to figure out what you are thinking about." I try to spin around, but Kaiden's hand settled on my stomach. *"What are you thinking about?"*

"I started putting these lights in the window and I was watching the people walk by. It came to me that I don't want to live in the city anymore."

"And where do you want to live?"

"I'm not sure, but I want to be surrounded by nature. To be able to go outside and smell the flowers or the change of the leaves, instead of the stale air in the city."

"Sounds lovely. We can start looking after the

holidays for some land to build on."

"Really?"

"Absolutely!"

I spin around and get up on my tiptoes and kiss him. *"Thank you."*

"Are you about done here?"

"Why have you missed me?"

"Yes, and I want to take you somewhere to show you just how much."

"How did you know I was here?"

"You texted me."

I look past Kaiden to Porter acting like he's minding his own business. He winks at me. Kaiden looks as well and snickers. Porter waves all impressed with himself.

"I just need to get my jacket."

"Actually, where we are going you need a change of clothes. I'll help you pick something out."

My curiosity is going nuts. Kaiden is giving me no hints as to where he's taking me. I do like the lingerie he picked out for me to wear. It is comfortable under the sexy little Christmas green dress he chose, as well. I get a pair of heels off the shelf. I reach for my jacket and he tells me there's been a delivery out front for me. I smile. I am feeling tonight is going to be incredible already.

CHAPTER NINE
KAIDEN

My palms tingle the second I see Ciara in the white fur coat I bought her. She is absolutely stunning. I've got to be the luckiest man on earth to be this blessed to have this woman in my life. I gave her my arm and her small hand gripped onto my inner elbow. We head for the exit and Porter stops us.

"Wait," he calls out, *"let me get a picture of you two all decked out and ready to show New York people how it's done."*

Ciara moves closer to me, leaning her head on my shoulder. Porter shows us the picture and we both smile.

"Best looking couple in the city," he says, *"Here, this is your phone."*

Ciara takes it and drops it in her purse.

"Thanks, Porter," I say as I hold the door open for my lady.

"Wow, Grams gave you her driver and car. Just what do you have planned?"

"Dinner is first. The rest you'll have to wait and see."

"Where is dinner?"

"Blacktie Affair."

"Wow, you are full of surprises tonight. First this expensive fur coat, then the most expensive restaurant in the city. What have I done to be this spoiled?"

"You woke me up three nights ago and told me you loved me."

"I don't need you to spoil me for that. Having you love me back is enough."

"Well get used to being spoiled, Ciara. You never know when I will give you more gifts or surprise you with something to show you how much I love you."

"I'd love you even if you were poor, you know that, right?"

"I do, and that makes me love you more."

"You remember I told you I was seeing Malcolm today?"

"Yes, I remember. Did it go alright?"

"It didn't feel good hurting someone. I'm glad it's over and I don't ever have to do that again."

"I'm quite glad myself you don't have to do that again." I smile, hoping she gets my joke.

"Well you keep showering me with gifts like this, Mr. Marcellus, I won't ever break up with you." I laugh when she sticks her tongue out at me.

Millie's driver stops the car at the front entrance and I open the back door, getting out first. Ciara takes my hand when I hold it out to help her exit the car. As we walk up the sidewalk to Blacktie Affair, the door greeter's eyes go a little wide at my lady's appearance. He recovers well and tells us good evening as we approach. The door is swung open just in time for Ciara to step inside first. The hostess is waiting at her station, I give her my name. Within seconds we are being guided to our table. I hear Ciara whisper under her breath that everyone is staring at us.

"Their attention is on you, not me."

"Oh I'm pretty sure it's the both of us. Why are they gawking? Is it my coat?"

I smile. My girl has no idea the heads she's always turning when she enters a room. The fur is gorgeous, but it's the woman in it that they see.

"People can't help themselves when beauty is before them."

We are shown our table and before we sit, I help Ciara out of her coat. The hostess holds out her hand to take it. I shake my head no. Not taking a chance on this coming up missing or getting something spilled on it. I have my reasons to keep it safe, so I neatly fold it and place it on the booth's seat next to me. We are given the wine list. I already know that Ciara prefers Moscato, so I go ahead and order a bottle that has been imported from Italy. I want her to get a taste for the real stuff.

We start reading over the menu. I hear Ciara mumble under her breath about the prices. Sometimes I think Ciara forgets she is rich. One of the things I love so much about her is the fact that she likes the simple things in life. Being with her reminds me money isn't everything. For many years, too many years, that's all I cared about. The more I made, the more I wanted. I have enough money to last mine and my children's lifetime. I'm ready to live a bit more simple, but nights like tonight won't be our last.

"Do you know what you are getting?" I ask.

"Not a clue! Half this stuff I have no idea what it is. When I do know what it is, it's something I've never had before."

"How about I order for us?"

"Fine by me."

Our house salads and rolls are served right when the waiter comes with our wine. I order the garlic crusted rack of lamb with roasted vegetables and baked potatoes. Ciara leaned over to tell me she's never had it before then asked if it's any good. The waiter smiled and left us to enjoy our salads.

"I don't know, I've never had it before either. I'm usually a steak or chicken guy."

"You like your pasta as well."

"That is true."

"I was thinking of the tuna. But then again why would I order it if I didn't care for fish? So you probably did good."

We fell into a conversation about my next business adventure ideas. I have a few rolling through my thoughts. Who knows, maybe I will test a few opportunities. I'm in no rush to get sucked back into the many hours it takes to start a new business. I'm looking forward to spending much of my time building the life Ciara and I want to live. That's the most important thing to me.

☙

Ciara and I were impressed with our meal. Now I am taking her to an art gallery. This is the part of our evening that I've been looking forward to. I hope everything goes as planned. It took a lot of planning this morning with a friend for me to be able to pull this off.

"We are going to an art gallery ?" she asks as soon as I pull the door open to Silvia's Gallery.

"We are."

"I didn't even know you could get in without an invitation."

"You can, but when there's a special event you must be invited."

I give the attendant my name and she doesn't check the guest list, but does ask to see my identification. I show her my driver's license, then she says enjoy our evening.

"So is tonight an invitation only night?"

"It is."

"How did you get invited?"

"My friend is the owner."

"I see. Very impressive Mr. Marcellus."

Wait until she sees what I have in store for her. I'm a little excited and nervous she won't go for my plan.

I find Silvia and introduce Ciara to her. Then I help Ciara out of her coat, giving it to Silvia. She knows what to do with it. After a brief conversation with the ladies, Ciara and I begin to take in the art.

CHAPTER 9

The first framed photo is a woman in a Santa outfit with a giant candy cane.

"This looks so real. Like I want to scream boo to see if she moves."

"Impressive, right?"

"Very."

We move along to the next frame. This one is of a man with a big bag of toys. The guy is of course topless. Ciara looks at him then pretty much is ready to move on. There are ten of these. By the time we make our way back to the first frame, her eyes go big.

"I knew it! These are real people!"

"They are. Pretty neat, right?"

"How the heck do they stay so still?"

"They only move when nobody's looking. Want to give it a try?"

"What do you mean by giving it a try?"

"Silvia has a display ready for us to use."

"We will be in the frame for people to see, and don't move when people are near?"

"Yes."

"I don't think I'd be any good at it."

"For fun."

She bites her bottom lip as her eyes travel around

the gallery. I raise my brows when she looks back at me.

"Fine, I'll give it a shot."

"Excellent. Our frame is this way."

I kiss her cheek as I take her hand to go to our spot. She giggles at me practically dragging her along. Silvia is waiting for us, just as she promised.

"I'm delighted you two are doing this. Your frame is winter wonderland."

I take Ciara's coat from Silvia. She'll need it in the fake snow. I help her into it and she is glowing.

"What are we to do?"

Silvia says, *"Kissing in the snow? Dancing in the snow? It's your frame, have fun with it."*

Silvia opens the side door for us to enter. Right away snow begins to fall and music starts to play. I step in first then offer my hand to my lady. I bring her to me and kiss her. I keep my eye out for any onlookers. We don't have any yet, so I begin to slow dance. By the time we have lookers, we freeze just as I dip Ciara. God I love her laughter. The people move on so I bring her back to a standing position.

We do this for about an hour. That's when I pull a little box from my coat pocket, and then hold the box out in front of her. Her hands automatically go to her mouth. She freezes out of shock.

"Love at first sight was something I never believed in until I met you. Yes, I saw you many years ago, but when I saw you at Vibe pretending to be an employee, you captured my heart's attention. Not once have I ever felt this way before you. I love you more than words could ever say. I want nothing more than for you to spend the rest of your life with me. Will you accept my heart?"

Ciara hasn't moved. I don't know if she's in shock or thinking because people are watching that she can't move. So I take the diamond heart shaped necklace out and move to stand behind her. I move her hair and slip the necklace into place.

Suddenly she spins around and crashes into my body. She kisses me, then takes hold of my face. *"Yes, I'll accept your heart! I love you so much, Kaiden."*

I kiss her with passion and love. Once our mouths part, I look at the jewel around her neck. She really does have my heart.

"Is this real?"

"The necklace? It better be."

"Not the necklace. Are you really giving me your heart?"

"Yes, baby, you already stole it back in April and I want you to keep it."

Her arms wrap around my neck. *"Holy shit! Second best day of my life."*

"Second, huh?"

"The first one is the day we met. I tried so hard not to fall for you, but I couldn't help it. You stole my heart, too, Kaiden."

We only spend a few more minutes inside the winter wonderland. I then take her to the next frame. I help her out of her fur coat, placing it on a white pillar prompt. I open the bottle of champagne and pour two glasses. Just as we clink our glasses together, we have watchers. Ciara and I gaze into each other's eyes until the onlookers are gone. Soft music comes to life and I bring my girl into my arms. As our bodies collide, we begin to sway to the music. I purposely picked this song.

"This is the first song we slow danced to at Vibe."

"It is."

"You are making this night very special. I'll never forget it."

"Neither will I."

Ciara's head rests on my chest as our feet slowly move to the music. We continue to slow dance through the entire song. When she looks up to me, I can't help but kiss her. Her tender lips captivate me as if it's our first kiss all over again. I never want to lose this overpowering attraction to one another. I would love to kiss this woman every day and have it feel like it does in this moment.

I reach for the tie at her waist to her green dress and give it a slow tug. Her wrap around dress loosens. Her back is to the display window. She gasps when I slip her dress down her arms. Her dress then falls freely to the floor. My eyes take in the lingerie I had her put on. I swallow. Ciara's beauty always takes my breath away.

"Close your eyes," I whisper. Her eyes blink closed. *"Keep them closed."*

I brush her dark locks back over her shoulders, my knuckles lightly tickle her neck. I hear the slightest inhale. I bend and kiss her flesh just below her ear, placing soft kisses down to her collarbone. I lift her, then place her on the pillar that I put her coat on earlier. Stepping back, I take in the most beautiful sight my eyes have ever laid themselves on. I move to stand behind her. Placing my hands on her waist, I slide my palms up her body, lifting her arms above her head. Then I lift silk lingerie top off.

"Kaiden?"

"Yes, Ciara."

"Are there people watching us?"

"Shh," I say, *"don't focus on anything but us."*

I tilt her head and kiss her while my hands wander and explore her body. Every light brush of my fingertips over her creamy, soft skin makes my manhood tingle with anticipation. When I slip my hand into the bottoms of the lingerie, her desire for me is known through her moan. Her back arches as my fingers tease her womanhood. My desire for her grows knowing I'm the only man that gets to touch her, kiss her, and bring this woman to orgasm. She's mine and I'm going to do everything in my power to make sure it stays that way. When I bring her hand to my mouth, her eyes open. Her eyes are glossy with desire. I kiss the top of her hand and then place it on her lap. Stepping a few steps back, I unbutton my shirt and remove it. She watches my every move as I remove the rest of my clothes. I smile when her eyes go wide. She looks over her shoulder. Confusion shows on her face. When she puts her attention back on me, I move to stand back in between her legs.

"I thought the hardest thing I ever had to do in life was to walk away from you in April. Then when I came to see you in June and had to walk away again after telling you I loved you happened. That was even more difficult. I don't want to ever feel that sense of loss ever again. For six months all I could think about was why I left the woman I love so deeply behind.

There wasn't one cell in my body that didn't feel affected by not having you beside me. It was difficult to breathe and function without you. Just to imagine the rest of my life without you I felt like I was being choked and life was getting sucked right out of me. Ciara, I love you more than I can ever put into words. I will spend the rest of my life… our lives showing just how much I love you." I get down on one knee and hold up the ring box I had Silva place here earlier. I can see her chest pumping hard as she tries to take a breath. *"There is nothing in this world I want more than to show you my love as husband and wife. Will you marry me?"*

Ciara's shaky hands cover her mouth. Her tears drip from her beautiful dark brown eyes. I wait for her answer as I take the diamond engagement ring from the box. When I take her left hand from her mouth, I hold the ring to her ring finger and slip it on, hoping her answer is yes. Her head slightly nods yes when I look at her. I get to my feet and wipe away her happy tears, then kiss her. Not once has Ciara looked at the ring I put on her finger. Not even after our mouths separate. Her eyes stay connected to mine. I believe I rendered Ciara speechless. I kiss her again and let my hands wander. I work her out of her bottoms, then tease her between the legs. I return her moans with my own as she strokes my hardness. I adjust her body, giving me better access to penetrate her. She holds unto the pillar as I thrust my hips, giving her what she wants. We made love to one another right there in the spot I proposed to her. This will be a night I'll never forget. Ciara is everything to me. I've never felt this whole in my entire existence. I'll love this woman until the day I die.

CHAPTER TEN
CIARA

Almost a full year ago I was dating an immature boy and now I am dating a mature man. A man that just asked me to be his wife. How have I become this fortunate to be loved by such a decent man? I don't fully know the answer to that question, but I'll be damned if I dwell on it. I'm the happiest I've ever been in my life. I'm going to count my blessings and continue to reap the benefits of having Kaiden's love. I finally love the right person and he loves me back. Our lives together are going to be the best days of my life.

Kaiden lifts my head and kisses me before he steps backward a few steps. I bite my bottom lip and take in the glory of having him naked before me. His eyes rake over my naked body as well.

"We should get you dressed before I have my way with you again."

"I wouldn't object to that," I say in the most flirty voice I can.

His smile tells me he's contemplating whether or not we should make love again. After all, we are in an art gallery. I suck in a breath at the realization of where we are. I got so caught up in the moment I forgot that anyone here could have watched every special moment we shared with one another. I glance over my shoulder and everything is dark on the other side of the glass. I feel relieved that it is dark. I jump down from the pillar and grab the fur coat to put it on.

"The gallery closed. Everyone left before I even untied your dress."

Phew! "That's a relief."

"You wouldn't want anyone to see us having sex?"

"Are you asking me that as a serious question?"

"More like out of curiosity. I mean they only would have seen your back."

"You'd be okay with it?"

"Yes, because it only would have been your back." He seriously is smiling at me and adds a wink in the mix.

"So it would please you to make love to me with onlookers because it would have only been my back? What if...," I say as I walk over to the window that

separates us from the other room and let my coat fall to the floor, *"I was like this, facing everyone?"*

Kaiden comes to where I am. He takes both my hands and places them on the window. *"If you are going to put yourself on display like that, you better show them the way your eyes half close when I do this!"* One of his hands leaves mine and cups my pussy. His fingers graze across my clit as he slides his hand up toward my stomach. I moan when they slide back down over my clit. *"Hell, we should show them the way you rest your cheek on your hand and bite your upper arm the more turned on you get when I spank you. Or maybe we could skip that part and show them the way your back arches when you want me inside you."*

I spread my legs, arch my back, then look over my shoulder. In a sexy voice, I say, *"Is this what you mean?"*

Kaiden's finger glides over my ass as he comes to stand beside me instead of behind me. Unexpectedly he spanks my ass. His other hand finds my clit as he spanks me again and again. I got so lost in what he's doing to my body that I forget I was teasing him. Without thinking, I did what he said I'd do and rest my cheek on my hand and bite my upper arm to silence my moans. My back arches more, showing him how badly I need him inside me. On cue, he fulfills my needs. The moment his manhood is penetrating me, he covers my hands with his, lacing his fingers with mine. He brings us to orgasm with each stroke of his glorious cock. This man knows me better than I know myself.

Grams' car and driver is waiting for us when we leave the gallery. We get in the back of the car, and I slide over closer to Kaiden and rest my head on his shoulder. I happen to glance at my left hand on my lap. As we pass under a street light, the ring catches my eye.

"Holy shit, we are engaged!"

Kaiden laughs. *"I believe we are,"* he says through his laughter.

I scoot to the edge of the seat and turn on the interior light. I look at my finger. Holy hell, this ring is gorgeous. And so damn big.

"Jesus, this thing is so… so big! This must have cost you a fortune."

"Worth every penny as long as you like it."

I can't tear my eyes off of my finger. *"I love it! I*

would love anything you gave me, even if it came out of a gumball machine. Are you sure about this?"

"What do you mean am I sure about this?"

"You didn't have to spend this amount of money on me. We can get something smaller and less expensive."

"Ciara, if you like the ring, it's what I want you to have. As I said, worth every penny. However, if it's not what you like, we can get you a different ring."

"I love it. I really do, but..."

Kaiden cuts me off. *"Then it's settled. Don't think about the price tag when you look at it. Think about how much I love you, instead."*

I leap my body on to his, wrapping my arms around his neck. *"I love you! I can't wait to be your wife."*

"I can't wait to be your husband."

We arrive at Grams' and Kaiden gets out first. The gentleman that he is, he helps me out. As we take the walkway to the mansion, I think about how I don't want this night to end. I'm kind of scared to go asleep to wake in the morning to see this is all just a dream. It damn sure feels like a dream.

When we reach my bedroom, Kaiden goes right to the bathroom. I walk to the door when I hear the water turning on.

"Are you taking a shower?"

He comes to me and unzips the fur coat. I didn't bother putting my dress back on, I just slipped into the coat and called it good. *"I'm drawing you a bath."*

"Are you joining me?"

"Maybe in a minute. I have something to do first."

He kisses me, and I feel the chill from the loss of the fur. I hold his hand as I step into the hot water. Before I lie back to relax, I put my hair up into a messy bun. My eyes blink closed and remain that way until I hear the bedroom door close. I peek one eye open and look at my ring. It really is gorgeous. I smile knowing I'm getting married to Kaiden. This is real, I tell myself over and over in my head.

❦

It is really late by the time Kaiden and I crawl into bed. I snuggle up close to him and lay my head on his chest. I've been thinking while I took my soak in the bath. I really want Kaiden to meet my father.

"When I was a little girl, I would imagine a father walking me down the aisle on my wedding day. After I had this fantasy, I would always feel like a fool for

thinking about my father in that way because I didn't have one."

"It isn't foolish for wanting something like that."

"In September I was with this guy Wyatt. He found my mother and he got it out of her who my father is. I went and met him back in October. I want you to meet him."

"I too found out who your father is, I met him the day you left Paris."

I am surprised by his confession. I had no idea Ciaro met Kaiden. I'm stunned that Ciaro didn't mention it to me when he came for Thanksgiving.

"I went to see him because I needed to know if he'd be open to the idea of acknowledging you were his daughter. He told me you already found him and that you had just left to go home. I missed you by a few hours."

"He was here for Thanksgiving and didn't mention he met you."

"Maybe he figured I had already told you. He probably didn't have any idea we hadn't seen each other since June."

"I can't believe you went all the way to Paris for me. You are just full of surprises tonight."

"Going to Paris turned out to be for me, as well. At first I just wanted to feel him out, then after

meeting him and knowing you two already were starting a relationship, I asked him for your hand in marriage."

I sit up and twist my body to face him. *"Are you being serious?"*

"I wouldn't joke about something like that."

I throw my leg across his body and straddle his lap. I bend over top him and put my mouth to his. I think I just fell more in love with this man. Just when I think I couldn't be happier, I am proven wrong. My heart is so full of love.

CHAPTER ELEVEN
CIARA

I've been wandering around the mansion looking for Kaiden. He wasn't in bed when I woke up this morning. The first thing I did was look at my finger to make sure getting engaged wasn't just a dream. I got out of bed with a smile on my face. I grabbed some clothes out of the closet and slipped them on. I damn near slept till noon. When I reached the first level I was greeted by the decorated eight foot Christmas tree. Whoever Grams got this year did a marvelous job. It's so pretty with clear lights, silver and gold bulbs. I peeked into the family room to see the tree there was left untouched. Grams and I always do that one ourselves. I checked in every room on the first level with no sign of Kaiden or Grams. My stomach growled at the aroma of something being baked in the kitchen. The kitchen is the last room Kaiden could be in. He isn't here either. It's just Katie baking cookies. I snag a chocolate chip cookie and take it to the table with me. Katie brings me my hot water and tea cup.

"Thank you."

"You are welcome, Ms. Verbank."

"Have you seen Kaiden or Grams?"

"I saw both of them a couple of hours ago. Haven't seen either one since."

I bite into my cookie and moan. *"Katie, I don't know how you do it, but you make the best baked goods."*

She smiles. *"Thank you."*

I make my cup of tea and Grams comes strolling into the kitchen. She puts her big framed sunglasses on top of her head. I laugh when she snags two cookies.

"Good afternoon, sleepyhead."

I lift my cup of tea to my mouth purposely with both hands. I just about spit my tea out at Grams' reaction.

"Good afternoon."

She whips her glasses off the top of her and puts them on. *"I need my sunglasses on to even look at you."*

She launches out of her chair and the next thing I

know, her arms are around me in a big hug. *"I guess you approve of me being engaged!"*

"I'm so very happy for you and Kaiden." She grabs my hand and takes in my ring after putting her sunglasses on the table. *"It's gorgeous."*

"He outdid himself."

She goes back to her seat and says, *"Give me all the details of how he proposed."*

I tell Grams how Kaiden asked me to marry him, leaving out the details of us being naked and the sex we had. Neither one of us can stop smiling. I asked her if she knew where my fiancé is and she told me he went into the city, that he had business to attend to. It sounded so weird to say fiancé, but I love it.

"Back when you dated Lincoln you put everything you liked in that app he had you do. I went ahead and ordered the invitations. They are ready for you to send out. I just need to fill in the date."

"But you didn't even know who I'd pick."

"We have plenty of time to get you married this month."

"Grams, Kaiden and I haven't talked about dates. I didn't think you'd really hold me to getting married so quickly."

"If you love him the way I see that you two love each other, why wait?"

"Why rush a good thing? I've been engaged less than twenty-four hours."

"I think a Christmas wedding here in the mansion would be perfect."

"Are you listening to me?"

"Yes! Are you listening to me? Ciara, this is important."

I am a bit overwhelmed. I sit here staring at her, dumbfounded. Why is Grams really wanting to rush me into marriage? The only thing that keeps going through my mind is that Grams is ill. She swears she isn't, but it's the only reason I can see why she wants this to happen so quickly.

I am about to open my mouth and ask her once again when Kaiden comes strolling into the kitchen. Phew! He'll help me to get Grams to see we can wait. I'm not totally against a Christmas wedding, but it's more like for next Christmas.

"Hello, beautiful ladies."

Kaiden grabs a cookie off the counter before he kisses my cheek and sits at the table with us. He eyes both of us who are staring right at him. He smiles and bites into his cookie.

"What did I walk into?"

"Grams thinks we should get married on Christmas! I told her we don't need to rush it."

Grams has no problem adding her two cents in by saying, *"Love is in the air. What better time is there than now to spread love and joy to others?"*

"Grams…," I get out of my mouth before Kaiden speaks, shutting me up entirely. I don't let it sink in to what he said. *"What?"*

"I think it's a wonderful idea. We love each other, so why not get married on Christmas."

"You are serious?"

"I am."

Grams is sitting across from me gloating. She's about to get her way, so she has every reason to sit here with the biggest dumb grin she's ever had. I narrow my eyes at her. I glance at Kaiden and he is waiting for my response.

"I'll be right back."

I get up and run from the table. I ran all the way up to my room and locked the door behind me. I then went to the nightstand where I left my phone last night. I swipe the screen and scroll through my contacts, tapping on the name of who I want to call. My stomach knots as I wait for him to pick up.

"Hello."

"Hi," I say.

"Ciara, what a wonderful surprise to hear your voice today."

"I did it!"

"Did what, dear?"

"I did what you told me to do and followed my heart."

"You found love?"

"I did. You have met him already."

"I don't know the other men, but Kaiden is a fine choice."

"He asked me to marry him last night."

"I am so happy for you."

I think I'm going to get sick. I'm so nervous to ask my father to be here. If I don't get this out, I will definitely be running to the bathroom. *"We are thinking of a Christmas wedding. I don't want to do that unless you, Molena, and Celine can be here. I would really love it if you would walk me down the aisle. If you can't because it's short notice, I can do a different date."*

"We would love to be at your wedding. I'd be honored to walk my daughter down the aisle."

"Really?"

"I'm sure we could come as soon as next week if you'd like."

"I'd love that."

"I'll make plans with Molena as soon as we are off the phone. I am beyond blessed you found me,

Ciara. You are truly a gift."

"I am blessed, too, Ciaro. I have to go share the news with Kaiden."

"I love you, Ciara."

"I love you, Dad."

I hang up the phone relieved that my father can come for Christmas. I am extremely overwhelmed knowing that there's less than two weeks to plan a wedding. I toss my phone on the bed. Then another thought crosses my mind, so I grab my phone again. There's a knock on the door, so I send a text real quick before I go to let Kaiden in. He brings me into his embrace once I unlock the door and open it.

"Are you alright?" He asks.

"I feel like there are a million questions running rampant in my head."

"If this is too much too soon we can wait."

"I called my father and asked if he'd be able to come and he said yes."

"So, we are doing this?"

"I think so."

"Why do you sound so unsure?"

"It's not that I'm unsure about marrying you, it's more like how are we going to pull this off in less than two weeks? I'm not positive we can plan everything on such short notice. I picked out basically everything

I would want already, but I did that without you. This is all stressing me out."

"Don't stress yourself out. I believe we can do this. I trust your judgment. Millie told me about the app. If you want we can go through it together."

I break free from Kaiden's arms. I seriously need to let this all soak in. I need time to think and de-stress.

"I need to go somewhere," I blurt out without thinking, this is what I need to do.

"I can take you wherever you need to go."

"I appreciate that, I really do, but there's something I need to do alone." I get my coat from the arm of the chair that I left there a few nights ago.

"Ciara?"

"Please don't be mad at me. I gotta go."

I get to the door. *"I'm not mad. I am worried, though."*

My cell phone chimes, alerting me I have a text message. I turn around and Kaiden gets it off the bed. He holds it out in front of him. I come back into my room and reach for it. Kaiden grabbed me by the shoulders and crouched a little to look me in the eyes.

"I'm not changing my mind about us."

"Then tell me what is going on."

"I just need to think and I can't do that when I feel all this weight on my shoulders."

"I can help you with that."

He drops his hands from my shoulders. I see disappointment in his eyes that I'm leaving. I kiss his cheek and his hands go to my waist, then wrap completely around me. I hug him back. I feel like such a jackass.

"Promise me you are alright."

"I changed my mind. I want your help."

"I went out and got us a few things. There's a box in the closet. I want you to bring it out."

He takes my coat from my hands and nods his head. I walk softly to the closet and retrieve the box. When I set it on the bed, I open it. There are all kinds of things in here that I've seen before in the building he had on his property. He tells me to reach in and grab the first thing I touch then hand it to him. I look everything over that's on top and end up taking out a black rod looking thing. He holds out his hand, so I give it to him.

"What is it?"

"My turn." He reaches in and brings out a silk strap. *"Perfect."* Kaiden takes my hand and leads me to the center of the room. *"Stress is the last thing that's going to be on your mind in a minute,"* he says,

taking off my shirt. *"You want all of me. All of my lifestyle. I'm going to give you all of me."* He tugs my pants down my legs, then lifts each foot out. *"Kneel, Ciara."*

I search his face to see if he's being serious. His brows rise as I do. He's definitely serious, I think to myself. I slowly kneel before him and then look up at him, towering over me. I wait to see what is next. Kaiden brings the strap to my eyes and ties it behind my head.

"I am the type of man that will take care of you always, Ciara. If you are stressed, it's my job to help you work through it. If you are worried or scared, I'll be the one to ease your mind. You are my responsibility now and I will do everything in my power to take care of you. You will always come first. You are under my protection and you will do whatever I say so that I can keep you safe. Do you understand what I am saying to you?"

"I think so. You want me to submit to you."

"I do. I want to show you part of what that entitles. Do you want that?"

"Yes."

His fingers brush along my jaw. *"I don't approve of the way you were going to shut me out. You don't get to do that anymore. I'm going to make sure you think twice about doing that again."*

Kaiden kisses my cheek then my forehead. I moan when he puts his mouth to mine. I can sense that he stood up once we stopped kissing. He confirms that for me when I hear his voice above me.

"I want you to stay put and think about why you were ready to run away from me instead of talking with me."

I feel his presence leave. I call out his name and he doesn't reply. It makes me angry, but I don't move from my knees or remove the blindfold. I get angrier when I hear my bedroom door slam shut. Everything inside me wants to jump to my feet and chase after him, but I know I'll reap the consequences of my actions later if I do. So, I remain in place.

CHAPTER TWELVE
KAIDEN

I left Ciara to think. I know she needs space to think about everything that has occurred in the last hour, or however long she was speaking with Millie. After she gets over my leaving her kneeling and blindfolded, she will think about why she almost left. Hopefully, she'll think twice before she tries to shut down from me again. I don't have any problem with Ciara needing space when it's necessary.

When I got back from going into the city, it was clear I walked in on a discussion between Ciara and Millie. Once I learned that Millie and Ciara were talking about us getting married this month, I was hoping that Millie would tell Ciara what that is all about. It didn't take me long to find out, Millie kept her secret. It didn't surprise me when Ciara went running from the kitchen very much. What did surprise me was that Millie didn't go after her to explain why the rush on getting me and Ciara married. I went after Ciara when I came to my senses that Millie wasn't going to. I'm about to blow this secret out of the bag if I must. It's a lot to keep from Ciara. I wish I didn't know what it was at all. The guilt is eating me alive. Millie put a lot of pressure on my shoulders. I can handle the secret, but I'm not comfortable keeping it from the person it's going to hurt the most. My anger at Millie subsided a tad when Ciara told me that her father is coming for this Christmas wedding. Then Ciara was about to shut me out and do what she normally does, hide. She was going to close herself off and let everything soak in. I need her to know that she doesn't have to face stress or pick through her mind alone anymore. I'm here to lift any worry or doubts from her shoulders. I know Ciara is the type that needs to let things set in her mind, but she doesn't have to do it alone anymore. I understand there will be times that I must let her do just that, but this is different. I have to know what she is thinking about us getting married this quick. I cannot ease her mind if she doesn't tell me what thoughts are coursing through her head.

Wandering around the mansion, I look for Millie. I checked her room, her office and all the rooms on the first floor besides the sunroom. Before I can go back to Ciara, I need to have a talk with her grandmother. The more I think about this big secret I'm supposed to keep, the more I want to share it with Ciara.

I find Millie in the sunroom reading a book. *"We need to talk, Millie."*

"Is Ciara alright?"

"For now she is."

"You can sit, you know?"

"I'm good. I came to find you to tell you I'm not sure I can keep your secret. It's wrong to not tell Ciara."

"I don't like it either, Kaiden, but it's the way it has to be."

"Why? Why does it have to be this way? You and I both know, she won't forgive us for keeping this from her."

"I'll take all the blame."

My voice rises. *"That's not how it works!"*

"I only told you so that we could make this wedding happen. Once the wedding is over, we or I will tell her. I promise!"

"Fuck, Millie, you have no idea what you are asking from me. This isn't the right way to start a marriage off on the right foot."

CHAPTER 12

"I know Ciara better than you do. She isn't going to hold this against you."

"Do you?"

"Do I what? Know her better than you do? I raised her, I think I know her pretty damn well."

"I see this conversation is laying on deaf ears. I'm going to walk away before things are said that we'll have to apologize later for."

I exit the sunroom before this conversation can get more heated. I am getting annoyed and pissed. Before I go back to Ciara, I need to figure out if I'm going to share this dirty secret or keep it between Millie and I. Calming down would be a good idea, as well. I cannot be Ciara's dom in this condition. I'm not about to take my anger out on her.

※

Entering the bedroom, I am pleased to see Ciara hadn't moved from the center of the room. I make my way over to where she is. Crouching down, I run the top of my finger along her cheek.

"How are you feeling?"

"Confused."

"Tell me why you are confused."

"I want to marry you. I have no doubts about becoming your wife at all, but hurrying our engagement doesn't feel right. I can't put my finger on why. There's other issues I have, as well, but that's the biggest worry."

"I would marry you today, if that's what you wanted. I want you to have the wedding every little girl dreams of. We can pull this off in the time we have. I just need to know it's what you want."

"I want it. I trust when you say we can do this."

"What other sort of things are troubling you?"

"The fact that I don't have girlfriends. I only have Porter."

"I'm sure Porter would love to be standing beside you. Just don't put him in a dress. I don't think he'd like that very much."

That makes Ciara laugh. *"You don't have a problem with Porter being the man of honor?"*

"Of course not. Anything else running through your head?"

"Nothing besides you leaving me here blindfolded alone in our room."

"I want to show you something."

I remove the blindfold from Ciara's eyes. She blinks a few times. I give her a kiss before I get my phone from my back pocket. Bringing up a video, I hand it to her.

CHAPTER 12

"I was going to wait for another time to give this to you, but I think you need to see it today. Hit play."

She taps the play button and a smile lights up her face.

"It's us at the gallery."

"It is. Watch all of it."

Tears fill her eyes when she gets to the part of me giving her the diamond heart necklace. When she gets to the part of me taking her dress off, she realizes we were recorded the entire time. She looks at me real quick, then goes back to watching.

"How did you get this?"

"I went and picked it up today while you were sleeping. Keep watching."

Ciara watches to the end. *"We are beautiful when we are together. Everything just feels right."*

"You didn't run away to have to let it sink in that I asked you to be my wife. You let it happen naturally. We are meant to be with one another, Ciara. No more trying to run off and shutting down without telling me why you might need time alone. We are in this life together now. I need you to know I'm right here beside you ready to be your rock."

"Okay."

"I left you sitting here blindfolded and kneeling to teach you a lesson for trying to leave. I won't always

be that easy on you. The things inside that box I had you get out of the closet, I will use those things on you for enjoyment or even punishment."

"I want you to show me what punishment is like if I do something you don't like."

"I will, but not right now. I think we have a few other things we should get done before this day is over. Show me the app."

After helping Ciara get to her feet, I take the box from the bed and put it back in the closet. I decided not to tell Ciara this secret I'm carrying around. That doesn't mean I'll keep it to myself, either. I still might end up letting her know. The timing just isn't right.

CHAPTER THIRTEEN
CIARA

This past week has been jammed packed with getting everything ready for the wedding. Kaiden has been my rock through it all as he said he'd be. Tomorrow my father arrives with the rest of my new family. I'm looking forward to seeing them all. I am going to be asking my newfound half-sister to be in the wedding. My fingers are crossed that she'll say yes. We don't know each other very well, I'll understand if she turns me down.

I told Kaiden I needed a breather today, so he will be dropping me off at my store before he goes to the art gallery. I learned last week when he went to pick up the video that he actually bought the gallery. I'm excited for this new adventure for him. I am even more excited to see what he's going to do with the place once our lives settle. Whenever I get overwhelmed with wedding details, Kaiden and I take a break. He distracts me by surfing the internet for property. We have decided that we are going to build a home away from the city. We've been looking at land in the upstate area. We are looking forward to being surrounded by nature. I haven't decided if I'll keep my store open in the city or not. If I do, I'm hoping Porter will continue to run it for me. I'm not giving up my career, I'm just going to be doing it from home. Kaiden will keep me from getting sucked back into overworking.

I lean over and kiss Kaiden when he parks near the outside of my store. *"I'll be back when I'm done at the gallery."*

"Okay!"

I give him another kiss and tell him I love him before getting out. I stick my hands in the pockets of my coat as I walk the short distance to my store. It reminds me that I slipped a photo in there when we were at Kaiden's moms house. An idea stirs in my mind.

I unlock the front door to my store by using the keypad and go inside. My store is closed today. so I have the place to myself. I go right into the back room and turn on the overhead lights. I take in the smell and almost instantly I feel calmer. Before taking off my coat, I take the photo out and look at it, then prop

CHAPTER 13

it up on my desk, where I'll be able to see it. I'll need to buy a frame for it. I don't sit behind my desk right away, instead I go to the storage cabinet and get out manila pattern paper and take it to the drawing table by my desk. I start drawing out the new design. I won't be selling this dress, I'm doing this one for me.

When I am satisfied with the pattern, I get up and begin going through material. I have plenty of silks, but I don't have the color I am looking for. Moving on to other materials, I still don't have any gold at all. Eventually, I chose a different material and color all together. It's actually the same deep red fabric I used for the dress I made for Grams' silent auction. I glance at the clock. It's been almost two hours since Kaiden dropped me off. I won't have any time to start putting this dress together tonight. I told Kaiden we had to be home by seven for a dinner I planned. I may not even have any free time to finish this project until after the new year, so I gather everything up and put it all in a bin inside the cabinet. I keep this cabinet locked. I don't expect anyone to see it until it's finished.

I grab my coat and turn off the lights on my way out of the back room. Kaiden should be here any minute. As I wait, my nerves start to get the best of me. My fiancé might not be too thrilled with me later.

It's too late to change plans now, so I'll deal with the consequences of my actions later if I must.

I see Kaiden pull up out front, so I put my coat on and exit my building. I make sure the store is locked before I get in the car. The weather has changed from a couple of hours ago. The sidewalk is covered in an inch of snow and so is the road.

"Feel better?" Kaiden asks me while I get my seatbelt on.

"I do."

"Since we are staying in New York, I'm having my SUV shipped here. I cannot believe you own a car and drive in snow."

"A car has been fine. I didn't ever drive that much. I lived in my apartment up until a few months ago, I walked a lot."

"You will need a new car. Preferably an SUV."

"Okay."

It's true I don't really drive that much. I actually don't like driving. I would walk every chance I could. Kaiden kept his eyes on the road the rest of the way home. When we arrive, Grams' car is parked right out front. That tells me the guests have arrived before we got back. Kaiden parks my car in the garage. Now that we are home, I wish we weren't.

Going into the house, Kaiden says, *"I almost*

forgot to tell you. Sam got out sooner than he thought. He called me while I was at the gallery."

"That's wonderful news. Where is he going? The house isn't done yet."

"He's going to his mom's. I talked to Hank, as well and he is tidying everything up tomorrow."

We take off our coats and hang them in the coat closet. *"Wow! What is next?"*

"I need to go there so that I can check the house out and give Sam the biggest surprise of his life. Well, the second biggest surprise of his life. I know it won't compare to what the Innocence Project did for him."

"He'll love it, babe. What you are doing for him is remarkable, so don't downplay it."

We reach the family room and Kaiden freezes at the archway. If it was possible to see smoke coming from a person's nose, I would see it coming from his. Everyone in the room turns their attention to us once we are spotted.

"What the fuck is this, Ciara?" He looks right at me. *"Did you do this?"*

"Yes," I say, with a shy voice.

"I'll be in our room. Get rid of them." He stomps off down the hallway, heading toward the grand staircase.

"I'll be right back," I say to everyone in the room.

I chase after Kaiden. He doesn't stop when I call out his name. I didn't think he'd like this very much, but I didn't think he'd react this badly, either. I jump when the bedroom door gets slammed in my face. I take in a deep breath before I turn the knob to enter my room, our room.

"Why the fuck are they here?"

"Because I asked them to come. I think it's time to move forward."

"Maybe I don't want to do that. You had no right to go behind my back."

"Oh you mean like how you did by going to see my father to check him out before you were going to tell me who he was?"

"That's different, Ciara and you know it."

"How the hell is that different?"

"Your father didn't know about you!"

"Neither did yours for many years. Your mother kept you from him."

"Am I supposed to feel sorry for him? He kept my brother from her."

"No, I don't think you should feel sorry for him. I asked him here for you two to have a fresh start. Not only with your father, but with your brother as well."

CHAPTER 13

Kaiden is madder than I thought he'd be. I stand here with my arms crossed over my chest, watching him pacing the floor.

"Unfuckingbelievable!"

"Kaiden, they wouldn't be here if they didn't want to know you. Your father wants to be part of your life. He knows he fucked up when you went to him. He's sorry."

"Did you get all that information when you were cozy with Gaetano?"

"Wow, Kaiden! Wow!"

I leave the bedroom and slam the door shut on my way out. That hurt! I could cry right now, but I must go and apologize for my jackass fiancés' actions. I'll lick my wounds later when I sleep in one of the spare bedrooms.

When I get back to the family, I make up a small lie. I tell them that Kaiden needs a minute to put himself together. Gene asks if he should go talk to him. I told him no and that we should just enjoy the meal that is waiting for us to devour. Maybe this will give Kaiden some time to get his head out of his ass.

CHAPTER FOURTEEN
KAIDEN

I am fuming! I cannot believe that Gene and Gaetano had the audacity to show their faces here. What in the world did they say to Ciara to get her to believe they want to be part of my life? Gene thought I was a goddamn con artist, for Christ sake! Then he thought he could buy me! Gaetano and I have nothing in common. He looks at me as if I'm this pathetic poor boy who had a horrible life. I don't need his sympathetic looks staring me in the face. I washed my hands of them both. My mother did the same thing once Gene took her to court for custody. What she did was wrong, but she did what she thought was right to keep one of her babies. I'm glad I was raised by my mom and not him. I never had him in my life and I don't need him now. I should march my ass down there and tell them to their faces. With any luck, they got the hint and left on their own.

CHAPTER 14

I storm out of the bedroom and go down to the first level. I go to the family room and nobody is there. My shoulders relax for a second. Then I hear voices coming from the formal dining room. I fist my palms. Ciara didn't get rid of them? She instead went and had them stay for dinner? Why is she defying me like this? I step into the dining room and Ciara sees me first. She narrows her eyes at me. I come further into the room.

"I don't know what you two put in my fiancé's head to get her to invite you here, but I'm not buying your bullshit. I don't want anything to do with either one of you. Stay away from us, especially, stay away from Ciara."

Ciara pushes her chair out from under the table, throws her cloth napkin on top of her plate and says, *"I'm sorry my fiancé is being a rude jackass. I thought I could invite you here to give you all an opportunity to get to know each other for real this time. I'm really sorry."*

She runs from the table. Gene and Gaetano stare at her while she leaves. I try to stop her when she runs past me, but she breaks free. I turn my attention back to the room. Why are they still here? Pompous assholes! I'm sure they are loving every second of this train wreck. Don't they get the hint that they aren't wanted here?

Millie breaks the silence. *"Kaiden, this is my home and you don't get to treat guests in my home the way you just have. My granddaughter that you hurt is probably crying and you did that to her. I suggest you make this right."*

Gaetano stands. *"You are a fool. You let your hatred toward us hurt the woman you say you love. Ciara loves you, you asshole. She invited us here because she loves you deep enough to fix what's broken inside you."*

"I'm not broken!"

"No? I am. I was robbed by not knowing my real mother and it bothers me. It eats me alive that I never had the chance to know her. I never got to know what she smells like, how she laughs, what her voice sounded like. Would she bring me chicken soup if I was sick? You have a chance to know your father and get any question you may have had growing up, answered. I can only know our mother through you and we can't even try to be friends."

"We did and it didn't work. We may be twins, but are two very different people."

"I thought that too until Ciara showed me differently." He walks past me, then says, *"You are a*

very lucky man, Kaiden. Ciara is an amazing woman."

I take the back way upstairs to avoid Millie showing Gene and Gaetano out. I fucked up and I need to fix it right now. I took my anger toward my father and brother out on the wrong person.

I try to enter our bedroom, but the door is locked. I knock on it. *"Ciara, please let me in."* Nothing! I knock again. *"I fucked up. Let me in so that I can apologize."*

Ciara doesn't say a word or let me in. Fuck! I royally messed up. I hurt the one person I never wanted to hurt. I'm an idiot. I put my back to the door and slid to the floor. I'm not moving until she opens this damn door.

I lean my head back and stare at the wall across the hall. Ciara thinks I'm broken? I don't understand what made her think that. Am I broken and I just don't see it? I don't feel that way. I just don't see there is any point in having a relationship with two people I don't like. I am pretty sure the feeling is mutual. Once I cut off contact with them, I didn't see either one of them beating down my door to know me.

I run my hands down my face. I can't think about them right now. I have to figure out how I am going to get Ciara to forgive me for the way I talked to her. I can't let this ruin us. If I lose Ciara, I will most definitely be broken. I close my eyes and think.

⁂

I jump to my feet when I hear Ciara scream and start pounding on the door for her to let me. The room has been silent for hours. I panic when she doesn't let me in. I do the only thing I can think of and kick the door in. Ciara is curled up on the bed in a ball. The side of her fist pounds on the mattress as weeps. I've never heard a woman cry like this before. I run to the bed and take her in my arms. I ask her multiple times what is wrong. She's too distraught to answer me. I rock her in my arms and hold her tightly to my chest. I wish I knew what was going on. This is more than her being upset with me. Something tragic has happened. I can feel it in my bones.

CHAPTER FIFTEEN
KAIDEN

I held Ciara for the rest of the night. She wept continuously for hours. She eventually cried herself to sleep. She tried to get the words out about what happened, but I couldn't understand her very well. My heart feels broken for her. I couldn't sleep. I was afraid to close my eyes. In a way, I wish I was able to fall asleep and wish this was just a nightmare. Whatever this is, it's something bad. My girl is hurting and I don't know if I can fix it. I tried to think about what could possibly be wrong. Nothing good came to mind. In the pit of my stomach, I know one of those thoughts could be true.

I brush Ciara's hair with my hand as she stirs in my arms. I hear a faint whimper escape from her sleep. Her fist hits my chest and I just hold her a little tighter to let her know I'm here. I place a kiss on top of her head and she moves. Her head tilts up and her eyes blinking open. Tears instantly fill her eyes.

"It wasn't just a dream, was it?"

"I'm afraid not."

"I have to go."

"Go where, sweetheart?"

"To see my dad."

"Ciara, I can make the arrangements to get him from the airport."

"You can't! He's not coming."

I am a little confused by what she is talking about. I am trying not to push too hard and figure out on my own what happened last night.

Ciara breaks free from my embrace. *"My dad..."* she breaks out into a full blown cry again.

"Your dad is what? Baby, I don't know what is going on."

"Gone forever."

She throws herself back into my chest. I hold her as tight as I can. It sinks in, Ciaro died. The one thought I knew in my gut, happened. I feel guilty that I knew this was about to happen and I didn't tell. I kept Millie's secret from her because Ciaro didn't want Ciara to know he's been ill until after Christmas. I'm the person who swore to her that I'd protect her at all cost and I failed her. If I had told her, she would have known this was about to happen. It wouldn't have been such a shock. She could have prepared herself for this day.

"I'm so sorry, Ciara."

I am sorry. I know how it feels to lose a parent. It cuts deep into your soul and you don't ever fully recover from it.

"I'm going to make all the arrangements, okay?"

She nods her head. I slip out from under her and cover her with a blanket. She curls into a ball and cries into her pillow. I leave her to go and search for Millie. I want her to comfort Ciara while I get us a flight to Paris and pack our bags.

I find Millie talking to Katie about dinner arrangements in the kitchen. I interrupt them. *"Millie, Ciara needs you."*

Her eyes show concern. *"What do you mean she needs me? Did you fix the mess you made last night?"*

"Ciaro passed away. I don't know anything else. She's taking it hard. I need you to sit with her while I make the necessary arrangements to go to Paris."

"Oh dear God."

She takes off out of the kitchen and I follow her. *"She doesn't know that we knew this was coming. I'd appreciate it if you let me be the one to tell her."*

She nods her head and goes up the grand staircase. I head toward the family room so that I can start making arrangements. Before I call the airline, though, I need to call Molena first. I take Ciara's phone from my pants pocket. I put it in there when I saw it on the floor when I slipped off the bed. I open the recent call list, I see Molena's number was the last call she received. There's no way to prepare yourself for a call like this, so I tap the screen and wait for an answer.

By the time I am off the phone with Molena, I know it will bring some comfort to Ciara knowing her father passed peacefully in his sleep. Although it will take time for Ciara to come to terms with his death, she'll eventually be grateful that he isn't suffering anymore. His battle was a long one and he fought hard to make it this long. His body just couldn't do it any longer.

I make the rest of the calls to get Ciara and I on the first flight out to Paris. I don't have much time to get us packed and get her ready to go. I have less than two hours to get us to the airport.

Entering the bedroom, I see Ciara cuddle on Millie's lap. Millie looks at me and I just shake my head. She knows I wasn't a fan of hiding Ciaro's illness. I go right to the closet and get out the suitcases. I start to pack our clothes. I have no clue what

I should pack for Ciara, so I throw in a bunch of comfy clothes. I get a suit from the closet for me and as I am going through Ciara's dresses, Millie tells me she'll do it. I go to the bed and tell Ciara she needs to get in the shower. She gives me a dead stare. I scoop her up in my arms and carry her to the bathroom. I close the door after I set my girl on the vanity.

"This hurts, Kaiden."

"I know, sweetheart."

"Make it stop."

"I wish I could. All in good time, it will get easier."

"Did you feel this numb?"

"I did. There are days that I still feel that way."

"We didn't get enough time together. My mother robbed us from having precious time with one another."

"She did."

"Your mom did that, too. It was different but all the same in a way. We are broken inside from the actions our mothers did to us."

"You think I'm broken?"

"It's one of the reasons I love you so much. You might not see it, but I do."

"I see. We need to get you in the shower."

"Gene is your father. You should give him a chance to be that before it's too late."

"I'll think about it."

I take Ciara's clothes off after I start the water. She gets in and she stops me from closing the glass door. Her eyes search mine.

"Get in with me."

Stripping from my clothes, I got in with her. Her hands go to my upper body, then her forehead falls to my chest. She burst into tears all over again. I let her cry while I wash her body and then her hair. I turn us so that I can at least wash my hair before getting us out. I don't know how she is going to hold herself together long enough to fly to Paris. I almost wish I had sleeping pills to give her. I put a towel around my waist and started to dry Ciara off. She takes the towel from me and does it herself. I peered out and Millie had left, so I opened the door, going out to get us some clothes. It's going to be a long flight so I get joggers for me and leggings for her, then each of us hoodies. Ciara picks up the dress Millie laid out and puts it back in the closet. She gets a different one and folds it neatly, then adds it to her suitcase.

"How much time do we have?"

"Twenty minutes."

"Did you call Molena?"

CHAPTER 15   117

"I did."

"Did she tell you anything? Was Ciaro sick?"

"Come sit for a minute." She plops down on the foot of the bed. *"Your dad had breast cancer. He's been battling it for six months."*

"Men don't get breast cancer."

"I have something else to tell you. You're not going to like it."

"Well I don't like what you just told me, so whatever you have to say can't be much worse."

"I found out he didn't have much time left days ago. I was asked not to tell."

"What! Why?"

"Ciaro wanted to wait until after Christmas."

"You should have told me, Kaiden. How could you hold this from me?"

"I didn't want to. I wanted to tell you. It felt wrong keeping it from you."

"Because it was wrong!" She gets off the bed. *"Everyone knew but me, huh?"*

"I'm not sure." Ciara starts throwing clothes out of her suitcase. *"What are you doing?"*

"I'm not going. I'm sick of being in the dark about everything."

"Stop!" I toss the clothes back in. *"We are going."*

She storms out of the room. I close the suitcases and carry them down to the front door. Ciara is standing there with her coat on. She narrows her eyes at me. Her foot is tapping on the floor. She's acting like a child.

"Ready, Master?"

I let that slide because I know she's hurting. If this were any other day and different circumstances, I'd take her over my knee.

Millie joins us at the door. She gives Ciara a hug but Ciara doesn't hug her back.

"Grams, cancel the wedding."

Ciara bolts out the door and Millie is shocked. I surprisingly am not shocked at all. A wedding in four days isn't going to happen.

CHAPTER SIXTEEN
CIARA

The past few days have pretty much been a blur. The news of my father's death has torn me up. Just when I finally get him in my life, he's taken away. It's not fair. I am full of grief and anger. I have been surrounded by people who all knew Ciaro. I only got a little bit of him. It breaks my heart that I didn't get to know him as well as everyone one around me. I am angry that they all had years with him and I had less than two months. It seems I am the only one who didn't know he had breast cancer. I feel like an outsider who barged in on the funeral for my own father. Through all these emotions, the one that stands out the most is the anger I feel toward my mother. Cassidy is the reason I only got two months. She knew all these years he was the one who got her pregnant. I hate her more than ever. I didn't think that could be possible, but it is.

I have been upset with Kaiden for keeping me from this secret of Ciaro's illness. However, I know he was only following my father's wishes. I can't stay as mad at him as I should because he's been here for me the most. He's taken really good care of me. He's let me cry, scream, or whatever I've needed to do. He continued to hold my hand and wiped my tears when I didn't ask him to. Hell, he's even made sure I ate when food seemed unbearable. I couldn't have made it through these last three days without him.

Kaiden and I have been staying in the guest room at my father's home. Every day I walk past pictures of the family. It makes me sad that I'm not in any of them. It's not their fault, though. They didn't know I existed. I can't help but wonder if we just had more time if I'd be on that wall as well. In a way, I am glad that Kaiden and I are leaving today. Being here has become overwhelming. I am starting to feel sorry for myself. I shouldn't be feeling this way. Molena and Celine are the ones who should be more hurt than I.

Kaiden carries our suitcases to the front door. Molena is there to see us off. I give her a hug. Her arms feel so welcoming.

"I have something for you."

"You do?"

She gives me a small box and an envelope. *"It's*

from your father. He wanted to give it to you on Christmas Day."

Tears that never seem to stop fill my eyes for the millionth time. *"Thank you."*

"He only got to know you a short time, but he was proud to call you his daughter. His love for you was natural and as real as it could be."

"As mine was for him."

"You are welcome to come here whenever you'd like. This is your home away from home now. I better be invited to your wedding once you have a new date."

"Of course you will be."

Molena gives me another hug then hugs Kaiden. We go out and get into a cab. I take one last look at Ciaro's home. I will come back, but my heart has to heal first.

Kaiden puts his arm around my shoulder and I rest my head on his shoulder. He asks if I'm alright and I shake my head yes. I'm not really alright, but he knows that. I'm not sure I'll fully be alright again. I believe Kaiden when he says the loss will always be there, but it won't hurt as much as time passes.

We arrived at the airport and board our plane. By the time we get home, it will be six in the evening. Tomorrow is Christmas. It doesn't feel like it at all.

Tomorrow was supposed to be one of the best days of my life, but we canceled the wedding. I was angry when I said to cancel it. I'm actually really glad Kaiden and Grams listened to me. I don't feel it's the right moment to get married. It wouldn't feel right doing it when Ciaro just died.

"I have a surprise for you. I think it will cheer you up a little."

"What is it?"

"You'll see. For now, just try and relax."

I hook my arms around his and lean against him. We have a long flight and catching up on some lost sleep might do me some good. Closing my eyes, I try to only think happy thoughts.

❧

We land in Vegas and I am quite surprised by this. My first thought was that Kaiden was going to take me to the real Vibe. But when we get in a rental and don't go near the strip. I had a second thought that he came to his senses and is going to try and know Gene and Gaetano. I am wrong again. The drive is too long.

"Where are we going?"

"It's Christmas Eve!"

"Well I know that." He just laughs at me and keeps driving.

What felt like the longest drive ever we finally reached our destination. Kaiden is smiling ear to ear when I glance at him. We are at his mom's. We get out and go into the house. Hank and his crew did an amazing job. This house has truly been transformed.

There's a knock on the door. *"Perfect timing,"* Kaiden says.

He goes to the door and opens it. They embrace each other in a hug. *"God, I thought I came to the wrong place,"* the man says.

The man who I assume is Sam comes in with a woman and a toddler. His eyes travel all over the renovations, taking in the change since the last time he was here.

Kaiden introduced us to one another. This is the first real smile I've had in days. I am so very grateful Kaiden brought me here to witness this wonderful moment.

"The day you were sentenced to life in prison, it broke my heart. I knew you weren't the man who could commit the crime they tried to pin on you. You had three years of your life taken away. Years that you missed with your family." Kaiden takes Sam's hand and places the keys to the house in his palm. *"This is*

a fresh start for you. I hope you share love, laughter, and happiness together in this house as a family."

There isn't a dry eye in the house. Sam is speechless as he hugs Kaiden. When he can form words, he says, *"Wow, I can't believe this. I don't know what to say except thank you."*

"You deserve this, my friend."

We don't stay much longer. Kaiden told Sam we have a flight to catch. I am ready to go home. Tomorrow is Christmas and I just want to spend it with Kaiden and Grams. I know it won't be easy. After tonight, I am hopeful that my heart can begin to heal.

CHAPTER SEVENTEEN
CIARA

Kaiden and I got home at two in the morning. We went right to bed. Both of us were exhausted from traveling, so we slept in late. It's hard to believe it is Christmas, let alone the day we were going to get married.

I woke up before Kaiden did. I just laid in bed watching him sleep until he blinked his eyes open. A little part of me is sad that we won't become husband and wife today. Another part of me is okay with waiting. I want the day we get married to be happy times. My heart is in too much pain to be fully happy.

My fiancé jumps out of bed when he sees how late it is. He leaned over the bed and kissed me, then told me we had to get up. I tried to protest and told him to get back in bed.

"It's Christmas and the morning is about to be over with. We need to shower."

"For someone who doesn't like Christmas very much you seem too eager. Besides, the gifts aren't going anywhere."

"You are right, they aren't going anywhere. But your gift is about to be here in an hour."

"Huh?"

"Get out of bed, Ciara." He whips the blankets off me.

"Yes, Sir!"

I get off the bed and he throws me over his shoulder, carrying me to the bathroom. I smack his ass as I tell him to put me down. The shower water turns on and he steps in. The hot water covers my bare ass. I yelped when his palm spanked my wet butt. Putting me to my feet, he laughs when I give him a look. He hands me the body wash. I take it and put a bunch in my hand and begin rubbing it all over my body. I moan when my hands slide over my breasts. When I reach out with soapy hands, he doesn't protest when I start stroking his cock. I get down on my knees, letting the water wash away the soap before I take him in my mouth. My lips stroke his shaft. I take him to the back of my mouth and back out. Giving him pleasure with my mouth turns me on. My womanhood tingles with want. Kaiden fists my hair as he takes control from me. I am rewarded with his release. This only makes me want him that much more. I sat up a little straighter, looking him in the eyes, I put a hand between my legs. He lifts me to my feet, spins me around and puts his arms around me. I close my eyes when his hands explore my wet body. I moan when his fingers enter my pussy. My desire for him to be inside me grows. I want him to fuck me hard, right here and right now. But he doesn't do that. He continues finger fucking me until I orgasm. Although the orgasm was good, I want more.

"I'll give you what you want later. Christmas is waiting." He puts the shampoo bottle in my hand and I roll my eyes.

After we finish our showers, Kaiden gets dressed in jeans and a nice tan sweater. I wear the same, except my sweater is white. I do my hair while he trims his beard. Just before we are ready to go down to celebrate Christmas, I go to my suitcase to get out the shoes I want to wear. I see the small box and envelope that Molena gave me just before we left Paris. My heart sinks to my toes.

"Do you want to open it?"

I shake my head yes. I take the gift wrapped box and envelope to the bed. I start to unwrap it. My heart is beating a mile a minute. Kaiden rubs my back. I open the box and inside is a hair clip. It's so beautiful. My eyes are watery.

"Can you read this to me?"

"Of course." Kaiden rips the envelope open and unfolds a letter. *"My dearest Ciara, if you are reading this, it means that I didn't make it long enough to give you the hair clip in person. I know you are probably wondering why I didn't tell you I'm sick. I wanted to tell you, but I was so overjoyed that you came into my life that I couldn't get the words out. I was planning on telling you, then you asked me to walk you down the aisle to the man of your dreams. I didn't want to tarnish such a happy moment by adding sadness to your heart. I decided to wait until after the wedding.*

The past few days my illness has taken a turn. I am more fatigued than ever before. These past few days I feel myself slipping away. I pray that this isn't it. I want to be by your side, giving you to Kaiden. I have no doubt in my mind that you followed your heart. I am proud to welcome him into the family. He is honorable, caring, and everything a father would want in a man for his daughter.

I love you, Ciara. You have given me nothing but joy these past few months. Our time together is too short. I wish that we could have more time. I am forever grateful that we got what time we did have. I know that you may carry hurt and anger toward your mother for keeping us apart. I ask that you let it go. You are too sweet to have her put hate in your heart. I have made peace with what she has done to us. What she stole from us. I hope you only let love fill your heart.

I will love you from the afterlife and be by your side every step you take in life. Love, your father."

I am sobbing. My father's words have touched my soul. He is everything I prayed he'd be like. I feel closer to him than ever. I will forever love him.

Kaiden turns my head to look at him. He uses his hands to dry my tears from my cheeks. I reach for his face and dry his tears.

"He's a big part of who you are. He may not have raised you, but you have his kindness. You love people the way he does. He's right. It takes a lot of energy to carry hate in your heart. I know this because I've done that for far too many years."

"Thank you for saying that."

"Do you need a moment alone?"

"No. I am ready to be surrounded by the love you and Grams' give me."

Before we leave our bedroom, I put the hair clip in my jewelry box and tuck the letter in the safe in my room. I don't ever want to lose my father's words.

We enter the family room and Grams is laughing. I smile that just maybe she has finally given into love herself. Gary lights up her smile like no one ever had. Maybe this Christmas is about seeing what love is really all about.

We join Grams and Gary. We open gifts and share a few cookies along the way. My heart is sad, but I can't think of a better way to heal it.

CHAPTER EIGHTEEN
KAIDEN

I have to admit, Ciaro's letter hit me right in the heart. His words of wisdom that he gave to Ciara will last a lifetime. It will help mend her broken heart. When we joined Millie and Gary in the family room for Christmas, I saw a genuine smile return to Ciara's face. A real one that isn't for a show like she put on at Ciaro's funeral. She will have bad days ahead of her and days that she'll be just fine. No matter what type of day she'll have, I'll be here beside her every step of the way.

Millie begins to hand out the gifts. My girl tells me I must open the small one from her. I tear the paper off and open the box. It's an ornament for the tree with our names engraved with the year. I smile and tell her to open the one in her hands. It's a crystal ornament with our names engraved with the year. We got each other the same one.

"I love it! One for our home and one for here."

Millie clears her throat. *"What do you mean your home and one for here?"*

"We are going to have a house built when we find the right property," Ciara says.

"But I'm giving you this place. I'm leaving with Gary after the New Year's Eve event."

Ciara's eyes grow wide. *"Grams, that's wonderful! Where are you going?"*

"We are going to travel the world."

"Congratulations," I say.

"Did it stink in that this place is going to be yours?"

"It did. I just figured we can talk about it another day. Kaiden and I want to live upstate."

"The house is already in your name. I signed the paperwork last week."

"Wow!"

"I guess once you move, you'll put this one on the market. It's yours to do what you wish with it."

"I don't know if I can accept that."

"You don't have the option to decline. Merry Christmas."

Millie has left Ciara speechless. I sort of find that to be funny. Only because I know this won't be the last time today that Ciara will be surprised. I have a few yet to come later and one that I'm about to show her.

I take my phone out of my pocket and bring up a website, then hand Ciara my phone. She looks at it and she looks confused.

"What is this?"

"Our land if you like it!"

"You already bought it?"

"No, but I will if you like it."

"Where is it?"

"It's further upstate than you wanted to go, but it's on the outskirts of Rochester."

She scrolls through the pictures. *"Do I have to give you an answer right now?"*

"No. I have a few more days to let the seller know."

⁂

We finished with all the gifts a while ago. Millie and Gary went off to the kitchen to cook. Ciara and I are relaxing on the sofa. She has her head on my lap and the ornament I gave her in her hands. She seems more lost in thought than anything. I glance out the window and see it's snowing outside.

I hope we don't get too much. It would put a damper on my plans for later.

"Do you think Grams will marry Gary?"

"I have no idea."

"You know she's never married before, right?"

"I did know that. Do you think she'll marry?"

"I don't know. I just hope she gives in to loving someone. It's been a long time coming."

"Well if things don't work out between the two of them, we could always auction her off."

"It worked for me!"

"That it did."

The front doorbell chimes throughout the house. Ciara sits up. I tell her I'll get it. Katie has the day off to be with her family. I already know who it is. It's another surprise for Ciara. I think this one will make her very happy. I am a little excited as well.

I answer the door and hug everyone as they enter the house. I take their coats, then hang them in the coat closet. *"Thank you for coming."*

"Thank you for inviting us."

We go to the family room and Ciara is laying on the sofa. *"Ciara, we have extra family members joining us this year."*

Ciara sits up and shock is written all over her face. She recovers well and hides her surprise with a smile.

CHAPTER 18

Getting to her feet, she hugs Gaetano. *"Merry Christmas,"* she says to him. She then hugs my father and his wife. Telling them Merry Christmas, as well.

Everyone makes themselves comfortable in the family room. I ask how their travels went. Nothing but small talk, really. Millie and Gary have rejoined us for a little while. It's very weird for me to be surrounded by so many people, especially for a holiday like this. For far too many years I have spent this day alone in my big home in Vegas. I usually ate some takeout food from the night before and caught up on lost sleep. I was always eager for the next day to hurry up and come so that I could get back to the club. I am not about holidays. This feels right, though. It feels really good and I'm in no rush for this day to end.

Gary made drinks for everyone and everyone seems more relaxed. The conversation is flowing more fluidly. Millie comes into the room and announces dinner is ready. My family follows her to the formal dining room. Ciara grabs my arm to stop me from following along.

"Umm, this is wonderful and all, but when did you do all this?"

"One night I couldn't sleep when we were in Paris. I got out of bed and called my brother. We

talked for hours. The next day, I called Gene while you were in the shower. We all want to give this being a family a shot."

"I am so proud of you, Kaiden."

"Reading Ciaro's letter he wrote you, I know I did the right thing. Hate is too hard to carry in your heart."

"I love you!"

"I love you, Ciara."

"Let's go eat a family Christmas dinner."

She gets up on her tiptoes and kisses me. I deepen the kiss. We part mouths and laugh when Millie tells us to save it for later. Not a problem, Millie, I plan on exploring every inch of Ciara later.

꙳

It is later than what I wanted it to be, but that isn't going to stop me from giving Ciara one last Christmas gift. When I started planning this one, I thought it would be a wedding gift. It doesn't really matter what occasion it is. This turned out to be the right timing.

Ciara takes her white sweater off once we enter our room. She thinks we are settling in for the rest of the night. I snuck up here a few hours ago and put a clothing box on the bed. Ciara hasn't noticed it yet.

"There's a box on the bed."

She tilts her head and peeks over her shoulder. *"When did that get there?"*

"I think you should open it."

She shakes her head, but smiles. When she takes the top part off and moves the tissue paper out of the way, her eyes go wide.

"Wow!"

"Do you like it?"

"I do."

"Put it on for me."

She grabs it out of the box and takes it to the bathroom with her, shutting the door behind her. My hands tingle with excitement. Lingerie is just the first part of the gift. I cannot wait for the rest.

It takes Ciara a while in the bathroom, but when she emerges. The wait was worth it. Wow! She does a sexy walk over to where I am. I hold my hand and she takes it. I spin her around, giving myself a full view of the outfit.

"Very nice, but you are missing something."

"I can't imagine what I'd be missing."

I take her over to the chair in the room and pat the seat. She sits and I lift one of her feet in my hand and slip a shoe on her foot. I help her stand once the other shoe is on.

"How do you feel?"

"Sexy."

"That you are."

I get the fur coat from the chair and hold it up for her to slip her body in. Her brows rise. She wants to question me, but she puts the coat on instead. I kiss her hand, then lead her to the bedroom door. We take the hallway and go down the grand staircase. I open the front door.

"You want me to go out dressed like this?"

"I do." She shakes her head no. *"Be grateful I give you lingerie to wear. Next time you may not be so lucky."* Ciara swallows, then bites her bottom lip. *"You are stalling. Should I spank you right here for not listening to me?"*

"No."

She steps outside and looks at me. I can only imagine how cold the air is against the bare parts of her body. She overlaps the front of the fur. I can picture how hard her nipples have become. The chill that radiates down her spine probably feels like a thousand pinpricks. I help Ciara into my SUV. It's still snowing with no signs of it letting up. I am so glad I don't have to drive her car. This night is a long time coming and a little snow isn't going to put a damper on my plans.

I start driving and after a few turns, I slow the vehicle and change the radio station. I drive through the neighborhood with the Christmas lights that are in sync to music. Ciara lights up as I knew she would. She liked it so much, I went around the block twice.

"You like it?"

"I love it."

I pull a blindfolded from my pocket and dangle it on my finger. I drive as I wait for her to put it on. This time, she doesn't hesitate to follow orders. I drive slow on purpose. The longer she sits here blindfolded, the more the anticipation will grow. Ciara squirms in the seat. I bet her mind is imagining what I may do to her. Her pussy is already begging for what's to come. I'm in no rush to give her the orgasm she craves. It will be like one she's never had before.

CHAPTER NINETEEN
CIARA

I put the skimpy outfit on that Kaiden got for me and looked in the mirror. I couldn't believe my eyes. I feel silly with the lingerie cupping only underneath my breasts. I have never worn something like this that leaves my nipples so exposed. I almost took it off. I knew I would dissatisfy Kaiden if I did. I walked out of the bathroom embarrassed until I saw his expression. He liked what he saw. I instantly felt sexy. All the silliness vanished. I walked toward him feeling bold and confident. A person I'm still learning to be. I'm getting better at being that person.

When I stepped outside the cold air was shocking. The fur is warm, but I didn't button up the front. I held the front together with my hand. God my nipples were so hard, it almost hurt. During the Christmas light show, I temporarily forgot how naked I almost am. Kaiden distracted me on purpose. I love it. But then, he dangled a blindfold on his finger in front of me. Every cell in my body came to light. I squirm in my seat just imagining what he has planned next. I gasp when I feel the front of my coat uncover my left side. The car stops and but the engine remains running. I grind my pussy against the seat when he pinches a nipple. I sigh at the movement of the car. God I want Kaiden's hands all over my body. My wants are quickly becoming a need.

The next time the movement stops, the engine is cut off. I hear his car door open and close. My heart rate picks up knowing he's coming to my side next. The anticipation for what comes next is building rapidly. Kaiden helps me out of the vehicle and tells me to step up on the sidewalk. He puts his arm around me, guiding me to wherever we are going. The snow covered sidewalks are cold against my feet in heels. I hold the front of the fur coat closed. My body is warm, but the cool air sends goosebumps throughout my flesh. We stop momentarily, then a breeze of warmth hits my face. He tells me to step up as we enter a building. I breathe in through my nose hoping to pick up on a familiar scent. I have no idea where we are. I stomp my feet, getting any remaining snow off them. Kaiden removes the blindfold. I blink a few times to adjust my eyes. I scan the area and nothing looks familiar. It's just an empty space.

"Where are we?"

"To the public's eye, we are in the gallery." I'm a bit confused why he'd bring me here dressed as I am, blindfolded. And why so late in the evening on Christmas? He finally says, *"Come with me. I have something to show you."*

Holding his hand, we go through a door to enter a small hallway, lit with red dim lighting. My body reacts as it did the one time I followed him through a hall just like this one. My need for Kaiden grows stronger. I desperately want to experience everything he's held back from me before. I want to know the real dominant man that he can be.

We stop at another entryway. He unlocks the door with a keypad. I happen to read the words *Vibe* written in gold lettering. Once we cross the threshold, I see the display windows that were here the first time we came here. I want to ask how he transformed the space so quickly, but really, I don't care to know this second.

"There are ten rooms. One room is set up for us to explore my lifestyle. The other nine are empty."

"Okay!"

"I am leaving it up to you to pick one room. If that

room is empty, we go home. If the room isn't empty, we stay."

"Do I get any hints?"

"Use your instincts. I have all the faith in you that you will pick the right one. Take your time."

I study each window as if a clue is there if I stare long enough to see it. Nothing really pops out at me at first. By the time I look at the last one. The tenth one, I think it might be the one because it's the one that he proposed to me in. I keep that thought to myself. I start over with thoughts of me and Kaiden in mind. When I get to the fourth one, I think it could be it, but then so couldn't the sixth one. Kaiden hasn't made this easy.

"Feel free to think out loud."

"I think I know which one I'm going to choose."

"Which one are you going with?"

"It could be any one of three. However, I'm choosing the fourth room."

"Why the fourth one?"

"Because it represents the fourth month of the year. You were the fourth guy I met. I chose to be with the fourth man, so I'm choosing the fourth room."

"Very interesting theory."

"Am I right? Did I pick the right room?"

Kaiden puts a key in the palm of my hand. *"If you*

are right, I'll join you in a few minutes. If you are wrong, you come meet me out front and we go home. Do you want to change your mind?"

"Absolutely not."

"*Go and unlock the door to find out.*"

I watch him walk away. I'm nervous. It's not because I didn't pick the right one, I know I did. it's more about not knowing what sort of objects await. What will Kaiden do to my body? I trust him with my life, but still, this is nerve wracking. I'm about to submit to him.

I put the key in the hole and turn it. The lights automatically turn on low. I suck in a breath when I see what this room entitles. I go in and wander around the room, touching a few of the things. Most this stuff I don't know what it is for. I find myself turned on by the unknown. My body aches to find out what this world holds. I see a mat on the floor by the entrance and I think back to when he left me kneeling in our bedroom. I take the fur coat off and lay it across the leather chair in the room. I take my place on the mat and wait. I cross my fingers that I'm doing this right.

I don't know how long I waited for Kaiden to come in. Every second felt like it was a million. The touch of his fingers on my jaw made me forget the wait. He's here and I'm ready and willing to do whatever it is he wants.

"It pleases me greatly that you chose the correct room. Your theory on why I picked this room is correct."

"It pleases me, as well."

"There are rules in this lifestyle that you cannot stray from. Do you understand that?"

"I think so."

"I have no desire to change the way you think about everyday experiences. I am not going to control your mind. You will always be able to be who you are. However with that said, if I see you going where I know you will put yourself in a situation that isn't good or possibly dangerous, I will intervene. I will punish you so that you learn your lesson. I am your dominant and you are my submissive in the bedroom and wherever else I see fit. Do you understand?"

"Yes."

"You need to make sure that you understand that I will use objects on you for punishment or for play and it will probably cause you some pain. Some more than others. If at any time you think I have gone too far or you just want to stop, you will use a safe word, then everything we do as Dom/sub will stop. You need to

trust me that I know what I am doing. Do you want to go forward?"

"Yes."

"You need to choose a safe word before we begin. It has to be a unique word that you won't forget easily because it will be our word for however long we live this lifestyle."

"Have you wanted to punish me before?"

"Yes, when you were mad and sarcastically called me master."

"But that is who you are, right?"

"Yes, but you were being a smart mouth when you said it."

I try to think of a word. Nothing is coming to mind. *"I can't think of a word."*

"Close your eyes, take a deep breath, and say what comes to mind."

"Terminate."

Kaiden lifts my left arm and takes my hair band off my wrist. He gathers my hair, tying it into a ponytail. His lips kiss the side of my neck.

"I want you to go over to the cabinet in the middle and bring me the gift bag that is in there."

I got off my knees and tiptoed over to where he wanted me to go. I get the gift bag that is inside. When I turn back around, his shirt is discarded. My eyes travel over his defined chest. I bring it back to him and he tells me to open it. I reach in and bring out a thick leather choker that has metal rings attached to it. There are even diamonds to make it look elaborate. I hand it to him and he puts it on me. I don't know how I feel about it yet.

"Are you ready to begin?"

"Yes."

"Tonight is for pleasure."

I nod my head and Kaiden taps a button on the wall. Erotic music starts playing. It's not loud, just loud enough to be heard. The lights dim. Then he takes my hand and guides me over to the cabinets on the far side of the room. He opens one and takes out leather cuffs, putting one on each wrist. He then gets another set for my ankles. I inhale when he slides my panties off to the side and runs his fingers along my pussy. I groan when he takes them away. He gets something else from the cabinet and puts it inside me, moving my panties back into place. I walk with him to the middle of the room where he hooks the cuffs on my wrists to a bar. He slides a padded bench between us, then I am suddenly bent over it and the bar is locked into place near the floor. Whatever he put inside me starts to vibrate. I close my legs on instinct.

"Remember the black rod you picked out of the box from the closet?"

"Yes."

I hear a click, Kaiden widens my stance, then another click. I can't put my feet or legs together. I am completely at his mercy unless I use the safe word. I try to move, but I have barely any freedom to do so. My mind goes elsewhere when the vibration inside me picks up speed and something smacks against my ass. It feels small but hard whatever it is. The pleasure and pain mix sends every cell on high alert. My body likes it. I want more. I can feel my ass burning more and more with each spanking. My pussy is soaking my panties. God, I've never felt this erotic before. I can't fully explain how turned on I am. How badly I just want to have hardcore sex. I moan when Kaiden spanks me between my legs. I want to tell him not to stop. My words don't come. I catch my breath when he unhooks my ankles then my wrist. He helps me to a standing position, holding me up because my legs are shaky. He swept me into his strong arms then carried me to the bed in the room. His mouth is tender and loving on mine. His hands are soft upon my skin and they are missed when he takes them away. Getting off the bed, he removes his jeans. Putting a knee on the mattress, he slides my panties off. He discards the top as well by untying it. I wrap my legs around him when he presses his body to mine. Kaiden kisses me while penetrating me. His thrusts are deep and slow. Between him and the bullet he left inside me, I orgasm. Before the wave of pleasure is over, he flips me over. I'm on my knees and resting my forearms on the bed. I gasp when he enters me from behind, thrusting in me hard. The choker cuts into the front of my neck as he grips onto one of the rings. I'm a goner. I slip into another world as an orgasm takes over my entire body.

I don't know what happened. Somehow I ended up curled up next to Kaiden with his arm around me. My eyes are heavy. I feel the calmest I have felt in weeks. Whatever spell he put me under, he can do it again and again.

"I love you, Kaiden Marcellus."

"I love you, Ciara. I can't wait to call you my wife. Ciara Marcellus sounds perfect."

CHAPTER TWENTY
ONE YEAR LATER

The day is finally here. I am marrying my best friend, my biggest supporter, and my lover. It's hard to believe that it's been a full year since Kaiden asked me to be his wife. We have gone through so many changes in just one year. All wonderful and welcoming changes. We found the perfect place to build our dream home. It's nestled in the country, a few hours from the city. We found the land right after I told Kaiden I didn't want to go so far upstate. It's perfect! We can see the sun rise and set, surrounded by wild life. The fresh air is amazing. I have a shop on the property where I am designing new clothing for my store in the city. My online business has really picked up. Kaiden has the art gallery with the private club. Only members of Vibe know about it. He is in the process of starting a new company with the mixologist that worked for him in

Vegas. Soon he will have his own line of drinks on the market. Our lives have really come together. Our love for one another grows stronger every day. Marrying him today is the perfect way to solidify our love for one another. I cannot wait to be Mrs. Kaiden Marcellus. I also can't wait to share our love with family and friends. Grams and Gary flew in from their travels around the world. Molena and Celine are here. Porter of course is here and is a nervous wreck. I find that funny. Kaiden's family came last week to help finish up last minute details. Gaetano is the best man. Their relationship has been wonderful. They are realizing just how much twin brothers are alike, even if they didn't grow up together. Kaiden and Gene still butt heads at times, but nothing that stops them from being father and son. As I said, this year has been full of changes. After the wedding today and Christmas two short weeks away, the mansion will go on the market. It is sad that this place won't be in our family anymore, but it is time to move on. It is time that both Grams and I follow love, instead of overworking ourselves. We both have found love that has moved us on from this big ole' mansion, but our memories will always stick with us.

I look at the woman staring back at me in the mirror. I look the same on the outside but I am completely different on the inside. Grams' silent auction changed me. I learned a lot about myself in the year I dated ten men. I am not as naive as I was before. I have grown in ways I never saw coming. I will forever be changed and grateful. Without Grams, I probably never would have met Kaiden. I wouldn't be standing here in a wedding dress.

"Why do you not seem nervous at all?" Porter asks.

"Because I have no doubts about marrying Kaiden. I have butterflies, but that's due to being in love."

"I wish I had your vibe. I am worried I am going to trip over your gown and cause you to fall flat on your face."

I laugh at him. *"Relax, that won't happen. Everything is going to be perfect."*

"In case I haven't told you, it is a real honor to be giving you away today. I know I'm not your dad, but still, I'm truly honored to fill his shoes."

"Don't be making me cry, Porter! I couldn't think of a better person to fill his shoes. You have been my best friend for so long."

CHAPTER 20

"I've never seen you this happy. You look stunning in that dress."

"Thank you."

Celine comes into the room. We've been using the library on the first floor to get ready. I smile big. She wears the dress I started making last year. Red looks fabulous on her.

"Well, what do you think?"

"It's gorgeous on you."

"Do you think Kaiden will notice?"

"My fingers are crossed."

"I have something for you." Celine holds out a small box. *"Our father gave it to me when I went to prom. I want you to have it."*

I open the box and it's a hair clip. My heart sinks, but for good reasons. *"Thank you, Celine, but I cannot accept this."*

"Please! He'd want you to have it and so do I. He had it specifically made."

"Hold on a second, I'll show you why I can't." I go over to where my veil is and get the hair clip our father gave me for Christmas. *"He gave me my own. It matches yours. We both can be close to him today."*

We hug each other. *"We better get your hair done. In an hour you will be walking down the aisle to your heart."*

We hug each other again. I sit in the chair across the room and let the stylist do her magic. I'm leaving most of my hair down in loose curls. The hair clip that Ciaro gave me, will be pinned in the back, holding the sides back.

※

The butterflies are growing the closer it gets to walking down the aisle. Porter is losing his mind with worry he'll mess up. Celine has been keeping him as occupied as she can.

My attention turns to the door when it opens. Grams comes scrolling in, making an entrance like she always does. It gives Porter and I a good laugh. I can hear him saying *the eagle has landed,* as he's done so many times in the past.

"Ciara, my dear sweet girl, you are absolutely the most beautiful bride I've ever seen."

"Thanks, Grams. You have got to be the most Grandma to ever attend a wedding."

Her attention turns to Porter and Celine. *"Mind if I have a moment alone with my granddaughter?"* They both leave without a fuss. *"Wow, my baby is getting married!"*

"Who knew your shenanigans would work!"

"I knew they would. I am thrilled to be adding Kaiden to our family. Hopefully soon some great grandchildren will be added, as well."

"We'll see about that one."

"Seriously, Ciara, I am happy that you found love. Watching you grow into the woman you are today has my heart filled. I have something for you."

Grams hands me an envelope. I open it, taking out the fold papers. *"What is this?"*

"The company. It's all yours now. I am fully retiring."

"Grams!"

"I don't want to hear any arguments. It's yours. I know I'm leaving all my hard work in good hands. I have no doubt that the MV line will do marvelous with you in charge."

"I don't know what to say!"

"Say nothing. It was always going to be left to you one day. This way, I get to actually see it. The business, this mansion, everything is yours. I have all the money I need in my account and I have Gary. My life is full." We hug. I am trying not to smear my makeup from the tears. *"Oh, one last thing."*

"What's that?"

"I have given Kaiden strict orders to make sure

you two enjoy life. Work, money, and business isn't a damn thing if you don't have someone to share it."

We hug again. *"Love you, Grams."*

"Love you, too. Now, let's get you married."

Grams leaves and I go to the entryway.

Porter holds out his arm and I hook mine with his. Celine is in front us waiting for her cue to go. I close my eyes for a brief second, thinking about my father. I wish he was here, but his suffering is over and that is what matters. In an odd way, I know he's watching over us, cheering us all on. Celine glances back at me with a teardrop on her cheek. She feels his presence, as well. She starts to walk down the aisle that starts just outside the doorway. Porter bends and kisses my cheek. When we hear the music change, we step outside. I look up toward the sky, it's snowing big fluffy flakes. I wished for snow and I am getting it. As we begin to round the entrance for the wedding tent, the butterflies multiply. This is it! This the day I've been waiting for. I look down the aisle and see my man, my life, and my heart, I want to run to him. I see our family and friends... Grams, Gary, Molena, Gene, Madeline, Sam, and I even see Malcolm, Lincoln, and Jasper. So many more people that have crossed mine or Kaiden's past somehow, someway. We are surrounded by people who love us.

When Porter and I reach the end of the aisle, Kaiden wipes his eyes. He mouths the words *wow*. We wait for the ordained minister to ask who gives this bride away before Porter puts my hand in Kaiden's. Our eyes connect and stay connected. We wrote our own vows.

"Ciara, I first saw you at a fashion show. I can't even remember why I was there, but I remember your beauty captivated me from across the room. Meeting you at that time wasn't the right time in our lives. Then one day by chance, I put a bid in to date you for one month. That entire month was the most incredible days of my life because I fell so in love with you. I didn't know what I was missing or searching for until I met you. You are the one thing in this world that can complete me. I will always love you. I am looking forward to the rest of our lives as husband and wife."

"Kaiden, I wanted so badly to not fall in love with you, but you made that impossible for me. From the first moment I laid eyes on you, I wanted to run. Then I felt your touch and it scared the ever living hell out of me. I did actually run and you ended up saving me in more ways than one. In our month together we felt the words we never spoke to one another. It wasn't until two months later that we said I love you to one another. The thing that I love about us, we didn't need

to tell each other, we just knew. You asked me almost a year ago why I love you, why I choose you. It is a very simple answer, my heart isn't whole without. You filled a void in my heart and helped heal my damaged soul that nobody else could. I don't ever want to spend a day in the rest of my life not being your wife. I love you, Kaiden, always."

We did the ring exchange and then he pronounced us as husband and wife. Kaiden kisses me, not being shy about showing anyone I'm his. I am finally all his and he is mine.

He whispers in my ear, *"I lost my breath when I saw you coming down the aisle in your beautiful wedding dress."*

"You clean up nicely yourself, Mr. Marcellus," I joke.

"Are you ready to go celebrate our marriage, Mrs. Marcellus?"

"I am." He takes my hand and we begin to walk down the aisle together. *"What if I told you that you're not only a husband today, but a father, as well."*

He stops in his tracks. *"You're kidding right?"* I shake my head no. I have stunned my husband silent. He eventually grabs my face and kisses me. Then he lets everyone know the news by saying, *"I'm going to be a father."* The place erupts in whistles and claps. Ya, I have the greatest life and it's only going to get better.

T he end.
Ciara and Kaiden's story may be complicated, but there are nine guys that are looking for love. They will get their story's. So, keep a lookout for them to come.

ABOUT THE AUTHOR

Thank you so much for taking the time to read Grandma's Silent Auction - December. Word-of-mouth is crucial for any author to succeed. If you enjoyed the book, please leave a review on Amazon. Even if it's just a sentence or two. It would make all the difference and would be very much appreciated. – OXOX Michael James

Michael's Links:

Website: http://michaeljames-author332.bravesites.com/

ALSO BY MICHAEL JAMES

If you enjoyed Grandma's Silent Auction - December, you may also like my other books:

The Way We Love series:

Pink Skies At Night

Shadows At Night

Nights Are Unlimited

Concealed By The Night

Shattered At Night

Freed At Night

Winning A Cowgirl's Heart - Trilogy:

The Rodeo King

The Best Friend

The Fate Of My Heart

Winning a Cowgirl's Heart -Complete Box Set

Construction Vs. Corporate- Trilogy:

Unbalanced

Balancing

Balanced

Secrets Within a Club

Club Comrade

Revenge

Saving Club Conrad

Masquerade Saga

His Pearls

His Secrets

His Prison

His Games

His Moves

All His

Crime in Landkaster series

The Mirror

Times Like These

Lonely Road of Faith

Grandma's Silent Auction series

January

February

March

April

May

June

July

August

September

October

November

Lost Love Letter

I'll be Waiting

Before I Do

Standalone:

Toying With October

Pieces Of Me

A Christmas For Eve

Dom Diaries: Tangled Up In You

Christmas Scavenger Hunt

Blue Christmas

Stealing the Christmas Spotlight

Co-written with Jodi Fahey

Last Sheet

Co-written with Daniel Grayson

Inside the Storm

Manufactured by Amazon.ca
Bolton, ON